Shannon City Breakout

John K. Meyer

A Black Horse Western

ROBERT HALE · LONDON

© John Glasby 1962, 2003
First hardcover edition 2003
Originally published in papaerback as
Renegade by Chuck Adams

ISBN 0 7090 7251 1

Robert Hale Limited
Clerkenwell House
Clerkenwell Green
London EC1R 0HT

Typeset by
Derek Doyle & Associates, Liverpool.
Printed and bound in Great Britain by
Antony Rowe Limited, Wiltshire

CHAPTER ONE

THE HOT WELCOME

THE heat of the midday sun was an oppressive, stifling pressure that beat down upon Dan Trafford's back and shoulders and touched the metal rings which held his gear strapped behind the saddle with swift flashes of fire. Two days earlier he had dropped down through the tall hills to the east and entered the desert which stretched now for miles in every direction. The hot alkaline taste of it was in his mouth, choking and sickening and although he had managed to find waterholes every night, had refilled his waterbottle each morning before he had hit the trail once more, that had not been sufficient to wash the taste away. A thin film of orange-yellow dust lay upon him and the magnificent stallion he rode, dust which had worked its way into the folds of his skin so that his whole body itched abominably.

By the middle of the morning on this second day in the desert, the dust devils had begun chasing him and the conviction had grown that this was going to be an even more terrible day than any of those which had gone before. He had known it wasn't going to be easy, when he had deliberately chosen this roundabout route to Shannon City and he had had plenty of chance to ponder and ask himself if it had been necessary during the long, seemingly-endless, hours on the trail. To the north, the main trail westward into Shannon City would have taken at least two days off his journey and he would have ridden well clear of the desert, would not have had to endure the prickling, blistering heat and the discomfort. But his choice had been deliberate. Here, in the country east of Shannon City, danger waited. Word of his impending arrival in the territory might have leaked out and it was essential that he should arrive there indirectly. It had been a small strategem, taking the desert route, yet he knew that it was something he had to do. He fingered the letter in his pocket, the letter which he had received five days earlier from Sheriff Bateson of Shannon City. He had known Bateson for close on fifteen years, knew him to be a fearless and capable law officer; but the letter had puzzled him. There had been little in it which could tell him of what was happening there apart from a few brief words concerning a gang of ruthless outlaws operating in the territory. But Bateson had appealed to the Rangers for help and he had been only too glad to volunteer to ride into Shannon City in answer to the appeal. It had been Bateson's idea that he should arrive there without it being known who he was, and that it would be wiser to take the desert trail.

Now his journey was almost over. About ten miles further on, somewhere on the yellow skyline, was the dark dot which marked the position of Shannon City. Before then, he intended to turn north, link up with the main trail about a mile from the outskirts of the frontier town and ride into town just as it was getting dark. He allowed the stallion to pick its own pace, sitting tall and easily in the saddle. He was a big man, broad-shouldered with a certain quiet arrogance that showed in his craggy face and wide-set grey eyes. He carried his guns low and the badge of his profession, the silver star inside the silver circle, was pinned out of sight, inside his shirt. He wanted no one to know his real identity except for Sheriff Bateson until he had bad time to look over the situation in Shannon City and see how things stood there. Past experience had taught him that it was never wise to show his hand until he was good and ready.

Slowly, his shadow lengthened as the sun lowered and a cool finger seemed to probe through the dusty heat, cooling his brow. A little breeze blew up as he turned and headed his mount towards the belt of trees which showed in the near distance, indicating the position of the trail. A vast stillness still lay over everything and riding had become a dull monotony with no sound but the steady, drum of hooves on the hard sand and the buzzing of the irritating flies. He crossed the rim of the desert and began to climb towards the higher ground, through rough slopes strewn with rocks and dotted here and there with lone hackberry trees. He was nearing the crest of a long, low ridge when faintly on the still air he heard the unmistakable sound of shots, sharp and ominous. Swiftly, he touched the stallion with his spurs and set the animal into a faster gallop, over the uneven ground and up on to the dusty ribbon of the trail where it stretched away into the distance in either direction.

As he breasted the rise, his keen eyes caught a glimpse of a small bunch of horsemen riding hell for leather away from the trail, down on to the mesa and then into the desert. In the dimness of approaching night, it was impossible for him to estimate how many of them there were, but he guessed at least six, possibly more. They rode tightly bunched together; and even as he wondered who they were and what had been the meaning behind those shots, they had passed over the brow of a hill and were lost to view.

Something far stronger and more insistent than instinct told him that those men he had spotted had been the cause of all the shooting and that it also had something to do with his presence there. Half a mile along the trail he found the answers to some of his questions. The stage stood by the side of the trail beside a clump of hackberries. The passengers were all out, standing on the trail, two of them bent over the guard who lay in the dust in front of the stage. They all swung round sharply as Dan rode forward, dismounting quickly. Out of the corner of his eye, he saw one of the passengers, a tall, well-dressed man, go for the gun beneath the frock coat.

'Friend,' said Dan thinly, 'if you try that, you're a dead man.' His keen gaze swept around the little group, from the driver bending over the wounded guard to the two women standing close to the open door of the coach.

'Hold it, Bellamy.' The driver looked up quickly. 'I reckon he ain't one of them. Looks like a trail runner to me. Mebbe he can help.'

For a moment, the frock-coated man stared hard at Dan, then relaxed and lowered his hand to his side. He nodded quickly but his eyes still kept their suspicious look. He said bluntly. 'They may have had a man hiding in the trees, just in case they missed something. I say we don't take any chances with him.'

'Just take it easy,' said Dan quietly, walking forward. 'I saw those *hombres* just a few minutes ago, heading out into the desert. Seems they weren't here for the sake of their health.'

'You're darned right about that, stranger.' The driver pushed himself to his feet. 'Bret here got it in the shoulder. He's bleeding pretty bad, but I don't think it's too serious. We'll have to get him to the doc in Shannon City as soon as we can. Don't suppose you caught a right glimpse of those coyotes?'

Dan shook his head. 'Too far away,' he said thinly. 'Don't you have any idea who they might have been?'

'They're the same bunch who held up the stage last week. But nobody seems to know where they have their hideout. They always seem to know when the stage is due. We've changed the times more than once, but they always know where and when to wait for us.'

'Were you carrying anything valuable?'

'Sure thing. They got away with the strong box. Twenty thousand dollars worth of gold bullion in it.'

'They got plenty from me too,' snapped the frock-coated man thinly. His face wore an angry look. 'The ladies too were robbed of all the valuables they carried. I intend to protest most strongly when we reach Shannon City. I understood that the Wells Fargo offered protection to their passengers.' His glance travelled to the guard lying in the dust. 'One man isn't enough to hold off seven armed men.'

Dan nodded. 'Reckon the only thing to do now is for you all to get back into the stage and we'll make our way into Shannon City. You can put in your protests there. I guess the sheriff will be mighty interested in this.'

'The sheriff.' There was a note of derision in the other's voice. 'He's done nothing since these robberies began. Either he's in cahoots with this gang, or he's afraid to come out and round them up.'

Dan opened his mouth to make a biting retort, then thought better of it and remained silent. It was essential that no one here should know of his connection with Sheriff Bateson until the time was ripe; and besides, he had the idea that there was something at the back of the other's remark, as though he were still suspicious of him, and wanted to know a little more about him, without making it too obvious.

After the passengers had climbed back into the stage and the injured guard had been lifted inside, Dan hitched his stallion to the back of the stage and climbed up beside the driver. There were several questions he wanted to ask and this seemed to be the best opportunity he would have of talking to the other without being overheard by the passengers.

'You said that these bandits have attacked the stage before,' began Dan conversationally, easing himself into as comfortable a position as possible on the hard, wooden buckboard. 'Just how long has this been going on?'

The driver drew a hard, tight mask over his face as he urged the horses forward and the stage rolled along the trail. 'About three months, mebbe four,' he said harshly. 'This is the first time they've shot the guard. But it's always the same gang, even though they wear masks. They must have their hideout somewhere in the desert and some-body is slipping them information from Carson. Otherwise, how'd they know when we were carrying bullion or dollar bills in the strongbox?'

Dan said sparely: 'Just what is that supposed to mean?'

For a moment the other glanced at him out of the corner of his eye, then said quietly: 'I don't know what your brand is, mister. You seem to be pretty interested in this. Could be that you're in cahoot with those coyotes, trying to pump me so that you can get more information back to them.'

'Could be,' admitted Dan quietly, 'but I'm not. I'm headed here from Dawson Wells. But it seems to me that if the sheriff in Shannon City can't stop these attacks, then somebody ought to take a hand in it.'

'And you reckon you're that man?'

'I didn't say that, but I'd like to help if I can. Those bandits are like plenty of men I've known back east. So long as people, decent, honest citizens are afraid to do anything, then they'll flourish here and get stronger and more daring as time goes on. I call my own brand and if somebody reads it, let him read it right.'

The other's gaze travelled over him for a moment, and then, as if satisfied by what he saw there, the driver gave a quick grin. 'I reckon you're all right, mister. If you ain't, I can always get in touch with the sheriff in Shannon City and he'll know what to do about it.' Dexterously, he rolled himself a cigarette with one hand, then passed the pouch over to Dan. 'Help yourself, mister.'

'The name's Trafford. Dan Trafford. ' He accepted the pouch and a moment later, inhaled the pungent smoke from the cigarette, leaning back, his keen eyes quartering the trail in front of them.

The driver's eyes had lost their hard, speculative look. He said slowly: 'Three times in the past two weeks, we've left Carson with the strong box on board but filled with nothing but stones and paper. Each time we had a clear run through into Shannon City. It was as if those coyotes knew exactly what there was in the box and didn't bother to show up. The same thing happened when we ran through with half a dozen armed men inside the stage.'

'So there is somebody in Carson who knows your plans and gets the word through to them,' mused Dan. 'You've no idea who it might be?'

'If we had, do you think we'd let him stay outside of jail?'

'No, I guess not.' Dan's jaw set hard. 'What do you know about your passengers on this trip'? Are they all from Carson?'

'So they said. The *hombre* in the frock coat who seems a little too handy with his gun is Cal Caudry. He looks exactly what he is – a professional gambler. I got to hear about him back in Carson. The place got a little too hot for him and they were all set to run him outa town. That's why he took the first stage out.'

'And the two ladies?'

'The young, pretty one is Mary Stacey. Her father owns one of the biggest spreads in the territory. She's been back east for close on five years. When I last saw her she was only knee high to a grasshopper. The other one is Kitty Masters. She'll be running one of the saloons in Shannon City.'

Dan nodded. It wasn't likely that any of the three was the one who had acted as informant to this gang of outlaws, but it was possible that Sheriff Bateson might have some interesting ideas on that point. His first impressions that perhaps Bateson had exaggerated the seriousness of the situation now needed to be drastically modified. It was clear that there was a ruthless and well organized gang of outlaws operating in this territory and that it would need drastic measures to eliminate them.

Half an hour later, they rode into Shannon City. It was a thriving, frontier town, a little larger than most that Dan had known in the past and there was a prosperous look about it which he knew, instinctively, would prove an attraction to all kinds of outlaws. He had heard little of this town, but he knew enough about the gold mines which had been opened up in the surrounding hills and that Wells Fargo were planning to continue the stage line through to Copper Flats, distant from Shannon City by a little over twelve miles. It would make rich pickings for ruthless men, bandits who would move in before proper law and order could be established.

As the stage pulled up outside the livery station, the driver said: 'I reckon that if you intend to stay in town for any length of time, Dan, you ought to get yourself a room at the hotel.' He pointed to the opposite side of the street. 'It's the only place in town where you'll get a decent bed and meals and with more and more people heading out this way, I reckon you'd better move fast unless you want to end up sleeping in the livery stables.'

Dan grinned and swung himself down. 'I'll do that – and thanks,' he said. 'But what about that guard of yours?'

'Don't worry about him. I'll get him over to Doc Travers right away. He's a good man and Ben will be up and around in no time at all.'

'Where do I find the sheriff's office, just in case I do decide to look into this a little further?'

'You'll find it just around the corner yonder. About twenty yards down the street to your right.'

'Thanks. I guess I'll look him up as soon as I've cleaned up.' After leaving his mount at the livery stable, Dan made his way to the hotel. The clerk looked at him in mild surprise as he walked up to the desk.

'I'd like a room for a few days.' Dan was acutely aware of his appearance, of the yellow desert dust which still covered him from head to foot and of the two days' growth of beard. For a moment, he thought the other intended to refuse, but a sudden voice from the corner of the lobby said loudly: 'Give the gentleman a room, Clem. I reckon he could do with a clean-up and some grub inside him.'

Dan turned in surprise. The woman who stood there was large and fat with raven-black hair and dark eyes that swept over him appraisingly. He saw her gaze drop swiftly to the guns in his belt, but the expression on her features did not change and a moment later, the clerk pushed the book towards him, handing him the pen.

Swiftly, Dan scrawled his name and gave the pen back, picking up his roll.

'I'll show you to your room,' said the woman in a soft, husky voice. 'It isn't often that we have trail riders in town. Usually, they're just moving through, either with the law on their heels, or a bunch of outlaws looking for revenge. I wonder which it is in your case?'

'Neither,' said Dan quietly. 'Though we did have a brush with a bunch of coyotes back there along the trail.'

She nodded her head, unsurprised, leading the way up the side stairs. 'The Carron gang. You ask for pretty big trouble if you ever try to tangle with them.'

'Do you know anything about them?'

The other's scarlet lips pouted and he saw her dark eyes dart swiftly in his direction, as though trying to guess at the reason behind the question. 'No more than anyone else in Shannon City. They rob the stage and make their getaway into the desert. The sheriff has gone after them with a posse many times, but always they have lost their trail and come back empty-handed.'

She paused outside one of the doors, unlocked it, and then handed him the key. 'You wouldn't be wanting to go after them yourself, would you? If you've got that idea in your mind, forget it. You're a big man and probably fast with a gun, but you can't take on seven men alone.'

'I didn't come here to fight anybody, least of all an outlaw gang,' he said softly, pushing open the door and stepping through into the room. 'Right now, all I need is a bath and a good meal.'

She nodded but the faintly suspicious look was still in her eyes. 'I'll see that you get both,' she promised. She closed the door behind her and Dan heard her footsteps fading along the passage outside. Throwing his roll on to the bed, he went over to the window and pulled back the heavy curtains, looking out into the street below. There were several horses tethered to the rail outside the saloon on the other side of the street and further along, the stage still stood outside the livery stable. There was no sign of the passengers, or of the driver and his wounded companion. Unpacking, he laid out a clean shirt and a white bandana. Hot water arrived five minutes later, and he bathed, shaved and combed his hair, then put on the clean clothing, feeling clean and refreshed for the first time in three days.

Going downstairs, he found the meal already prepared for him. As he sat down at the table, he realized just how hungry he really was. Three days on the trail, eating nothing but baked beans and a couple of wild turkeys that he had shot in the desert had given him an appetite and he made a hearty meal of potatoes, cabbage and meat, followed by baked cranberry pie and strong, black coffee. Finally, he leaned back in his chair, completely satisfied. The woman came over, drew back the chair opposite him and sat down, regarding him curiously.

'I reckon you're wondering why I'm so interested in you, Mister Trafford,' she said softly, her eyes never leaving his face.

'To be quite honest, Ma'am, I am.' His eyes met hers unflinchingly. 'Seems there are several people who're interested in me. I'm beginning to wonder why?'

'Several?'

'There was a gambler on the stage that was held up just outside of town. A fella named Cal Caudry. He seemed to think I was in with the gang who robbed the stage. I've been thinking since then and it seems to me that the reason he made so much of that was because he wanted to divert suspicion away from himself.'

He paused, rested his arms on the table. For a moment, his mouth tightened, then he said quietly: 'But just why are you interested in me? Do you reckon I'm in with that gang?'

She shook her head. 'If you were, I don't figure you'd be here. But in Shannon City, we either get prospectors figuring they'll strike it rich out in the hills, cowpunchers looking for a job on the ranches around these parts, or just ordinary drifters passing through. Somehow, you don't seem to fit into any of those categories. I knew that the minute I set eyes on you. That's why I made Clem give you that room. I wanted to know a little more about you. It may come as a surprise to you but I have a big stake in this town. I don't want to lose everything, just because of a gang of robbers and outlaws. The sooner they're rounded up, the safer I'll feel.'

'I reckon I know how you feel. There's a new order coming to places like this, but it's a long way off yet, and men like these bandits are holding it back even more. The stage line is going to pass through Shannon City and the next thing, the railroad will be coming through. This town could become a big name in the west, ten times as prosperous as it is now, but the surrounding territory will have to be cleaned up first.'

'I guessed you'd see it my way, but if you're figuring on doing any of that cleaning up yourself, I'd better warn you right now that it isn't going to be easy. One or two have already tried it, but they didn't get very far. They headed out into the desert, trying to find the hideout of this gang, but we've seen nothing more of them. If you want my opinion, they're out there now, buzzard-meat.'

'Don't worry about me. I assure you I can look after my hide very well indeed.'

'Sure you can. But we've had a packet of trouble in this town and a man is liable to get a mite too cautious. That's the trouble with the sheriff. I reckon he knows just when he's beaten, but he still keeps trying. The mayor is getting up some kind of committee for forcing his hand but he's sitting tight.'

'You mean that he's going to take the law into his own hands?' Dan was openly incredulous. 'And where does he think that he's going to succeed if the sheriff failed?'

'Reckon he thinks the sheriff is too slow or too soft. Anyways, they're holding a meeting tomorrow night to discuss the problem. Sheriff Bateson has been invited, but if he's got any sense, he'll stay away. If he goes, it'll look suspiciously like he's agreeing with them and that won't do his reputation any good.'

Dan nodded. 'I'd like to have a talk with this sheriff of yours,' he said casually. Not by a flicker of an eyelid did he give away the fact that Bateson and he were good friends. 'Where can I find him at this time of day?'

'He'll be in his office, I reckon. But you'll get nothing out of him. He doesn't take too kindly to strangers and if your gambler friend has already had a talk with him, it could be that you might have some explaining to do yourself.'

'He may have, but I guess I'll have to risk that. Seems that trouble and I are never very far apart.' He pushed back his chair and got to his feet. 'Thanks for the excellent meal. It makes a welcome change after the grub I've been eating on the trail these past three days.'

'You're welcome, Mister Trafford.' She smiled up at him, the golden rings in her ears swaying slightly as she shook her head slowly from side to side. 'Either you're a very foolish and impetuous man, or there's more to you than meets the eye. At the moment, I'm not sure which it is.'

As he turned the corner of the street, Dan saw a tall, familiar figure come out of the sheriff's office and walk quickly along the boardwalk in the opposite direction. It was obvious that Caudry had not seen him and Dan breathed a faint sigh of relief. The gambler was the last person he wanted to know that he was paying a visit to the sheriff. Swiftly, he moved along the boardwalk, threw a quick look up and down the street, then pushed open the door and went inside.

The man seated behind the desk, short and wiry, with a Stetson pushed well back on his greying hair, looked up quickly, then got swiftly to his feet and moved forward, his hand outstretched,

16

'Dan Trafford. Thank God you've finally arrived.' He shook Dan's hand in welcome. 'From the description that my last visitor gave, I guessed that it might have been you that accompanied that stage into town, but when you didn't show up earlier, I figured I might have been wrong.'

Dan sat down in the chair in front of the desk as the other moved back around it and lowered himself into his seat. 'I got myself a room at the hotel,' he explained easily. 'Figured I might as well get me some place to stay before I made a move to contact you. I gather things have been pretty bad during the past few weeks.'

The other gave a quick nod, his brow furrowed in thought and lines of strain clearly visible around the corners of his eyes and mouth. 'That's putting it quite mildly, Dan. We've got a big problem on our hands here. You'll have heard some of it from the driver of the stage on your way in.'

'And from the woman who seems to run the local hotel.' Dan grinned.

The other's brows lifted slightly, then he nodded. 'Oh, Beth Allison. So she's been talking. She told you about Mayor Wayne?'

'I gather that he's called a special meeting and asked you to be there. Are you going along?'

'I haven't made up my mind yet. I wanted you here first. We've got a lot to talk about and I'd feel in a stronger position if I knew you were backing me up.'

'You know you can take that for granted. But if you could put me into the picture, I might be of more help. I assume that your trouble has something to do with the gang who robbed the stage?'

'That's right. The Carron gang. They moved into this territory about two months ago. I heard from a friend of mine that they were originally from Montana, but things got a little too hot for them there and they decided to move into new territory. They have a hideout somewhere in the desert, but so far we've been unable to locate it and it isn't easy to follow a trail through the desert. Besides, it's a mighty big place and there are thousands of places where they could be hiding out.'

'The Carron gang. Seems I've heard that name before.' Dan racked his memory for a moment, then nodded. 'I remember now. Jeb and Luke Carron. Wanted for every crime there is from stage robbery to murder. The last I heard of them they were operating alone. Seems they've picked up another five men much like themselves.'

'All reports we've had so far talk of seven men,' agreed the other. 'But they have someone else working for them in Carson. Someone who knows everything carried on that stage and the time it leaves. We've checked on the payroll of Wells Fargo but got nowhere. All of their employees seem to be honest and upright men. We could find nothing against any of them.'

'Yet they're still getting the information about the coach.'

'Everything they need. If we could stop that source of information we might have a chance to trap them. So far, we've had no luck whatever.'

Dan nodded and settled back in his chair. 'Tell me, what do you know about a gambler called Caudry?'

The other looked surprised, then grinned wryly. 'He's a two-bit gambler who does the round of the frontier towns. He was in Carson for a while, then moved on to here when things got a little too hot for him. He was here just before you came, protesting about the fact that he had lost everything of value during the hold-up and expecting me to reimburse him. He's a man who lives by his wits and from what I've heard, he's quite slick with a gun. There are four dead men in Carson to testify to that, although whether he shot them in fair fight or not is something I don't know. If he did, then he's a dangerous man to cross.'

'Think he could have anything to do with getting information to this gang?'

Bateson pursed his lips in sudden thought, then shook his head. 'I doubt it. He's a logical suspect, I'll admit. But he doesn't seem the kind of man to fit in with a deal like that. Could be that they robbed him though, to throw suspicion away from him. Guess we'd better keep an eye on Mister Caudry, just in case you're right, Dan.'

'Maybe the only way we can get at them is to play their own game,' mused Dan. 'At least, it might force one or two of them into the open.'

'How do you figure on doing that, Dan?'

Dan rolled himself a cigarette. He said tightly: 'Somebody has got to join up with the Carron gang, find out where they're hiding out and then get the information back to you. It's the only chance we have.'

'That would be sheer suicide. They're suspicious enough as it is and it would need only one slip and you'd be a dead man.'

'Sure,' agreed Dan. 'But somebody has got to stop this gang from ruining Shannon City and the whole of the surrounding territory. So far, I'm a stranger here and there are more than a few willing to believe at the moment, that I'm in cahoots with that gang. There may also be a way I can work myself into that gang.'

'It isn't going to be easy,' protested the other. 'If they once suspect that you're a lawman, they'll shoot you in cold blood. Believe me, I know the type of men we're dealing with. They're ruthless, vicious killers. Human life means nothing to them.'

'I've met their kind before – quite often.' Dan reached inside his shirt and unpinned the Ranger's star, handing it across to the other. 'I reckon you'd better keep this for the time being. The work I have in mind isn't the sort usually associated with a Ranger. When I need it again, I'll come for it.'

The sheriff hesitated for a moment, then shrugged his shoulders as he took it and slipped it inside the drawer of his desk. 'What is it you've got in mind, Dan? You can count on any help you need from me.'

Briefly, Dan outlined his plans to the other. When he left the sheriff's office, he carried nothing which could possibly indentify him as a Ranger. He still wore his guns

19

low, but to the casual observer, he was just a saddletramp, spruced up for his first visit to Shannon City.

Two days later, after deliberately building up the impression he wished to create in Shannon City, Dan rode out along the dusty trail, heading in the direction of Carson. All preparations had been made with Sheriff Bateson and he rode with the knowledge that if nothing went wrong, he would soon be joining the outlaw band led by Jeb and Luke Carron. When he finally left the trail through the greenness of the pine belt which bordered the northern edge of the vast desert, and came in sight of the straggling township of Carson, he felt a pang of distaste. The town was even more vulgar and gaudy than Shannon City, with its brightly painted saloons, the two-storeyed buildings which seemed to have mushroomed up almost overnight in every direction with no thought for proper lay-out or planning. It looked as if a crowd of people had arrived there at one and the same time and had thrown up a shack just where they had stopped.

Riding down the main street in the heat of the dusty afternoon, he was aware of the curious stares turned in his direction from the boardwalks. Here, a stranger seemed to be viewed with even more suspicion than back in Shannon City.

He reined in and dismounted in front of the saloon, tethering the stallion to the hitching rail. Deliberately ignoring the looks of the people on the street, he pushed open the batwing doors of the saloon and went inside. There were several men drinking at the bar and although few of them turned to look at him directly, he noticed that all of them were watching him closely through the mirror at the back of the bar, a mirror which stretched along the whole length of the wall,

'What'll you have, Mister?' growled the bartender.

'Whisky.' Dan pushed back his hat and watched as the other poured out the drink, thrusting the glass towards him over the polished bar. He drank it down quickly, reached out for the bottle as the other moved to take it and said gruffly. 'Leave the bottle here. It's thirsty riding that trail out there and a man needs a drink.'

The other made to say something then bit back the words and relaxed. 'Go ahead, Mister. So long as you pay for it, that's all right by me,'

The man next to Dan said harshly: 'What's the matter, *hombre*? You look kinda low-spirited? Met up with something on the trail?'

'Nope. Why should I? Just rode in from Montana. Thought I'd try a little prospecting. Heard that some guys had struck it rich out here.'

The man's upper lip curled as he snarled: 'You must be a stranger around here to believe any stories like that, mister. Sure there were one or two strikes made out in the hills over to the west, but they've been mostly worked out and those that still yield any gold are mined by the big syndicate in Shannon City, headed by Beth Allison. If you're thinking of cutting in on her territory, better forget it right now. She may look like a poor, defenceless woman, but I'd sooner face up to an angry rattler than her.'

Dan accepted that piece of information without allowing any of the surprise to show through on his face. When Beth had told him that she held a big stake in Shannon City, he had never imagined that it had been anything as big as that. Small wonder that she looked with alarm upon the incursions of the Carron gang in the neighbourhood. Once they started raiding the stages carrying the gold shipments east, she stood to lose a great deal.

'I did hear that there was a gang of outlaws operating in these parts? Any truth in that?'

'You mean the Carron gang.' The other's voice seemed to drop in pitch and volume, as if he was afraid of being overheard. 'You heard right, mister. Only it don't do to be too inquisitive where they're concerned. Just keep clear of them and you might live to die in your bed.'

'As bad as that.' He poured himself a drink and one for the other. 'Then let's drink to the Carron gang. They might make life interesting.'

'Don't joke about them, mister.' For a moment, Dan thought he saw a look of fear cross the other's face. 'They're bad medicine.'

'Then I'll do my best to steer clear of them.' Dan laughed, a harsh rasping sound that was a travesty of mirth. Suddenly he stiffened as a voice from the doorway said thinly: 'Just stand where you are and don't make an attempt to go for those guns, or I'll shoot you in the back.'

He rested his hands flat on the top of the bar as the two men came forward into the room, the guns in their hands never wavering from the small of his back.

'That's better. Now turn round very slowly. And no tricks mind. You won't find it so easy to get away from us this time.'

He forced a thin smile to his lips as he stared across at the man holding the gun on him. 'I ought to have shot you when I had the chance, Sheriff,' he gritted harshly. 'I always did figure that was a mistake.'

'You'll soon find out how big a mistake it really was,' muttered Bateson, moving forward and pulling the two guns from Dan's belt, letting them drop with hollow thuds on to the floor. 'We're taking you back on the next stage into Shannon City. Reckon you'll stand trial there.'

'Your jurisdiction doesn't extend into Carson,' Dan said thinly, easing his shoulders away from the bar. 'You can't arrest me here.'

'Don't let that worry you, Clayton. Everything has been arranged with Sheriff Gladwell here. You're in my charge now and this time, there'll be no chance of any escape for you. The jail in Shannon City was built specially to hold men like you.'

As he went forward, with Bateson's gun still on him, Dan was aware of the eyes of every man in the room on him, men exchanging glances as he moved slowly towards the door where the second man stood waiting. 'What's he done, Sheriff?' asked one of the men, seated at a nearby table.

'What's he done?' echoed Bateson. 'He's just about the

most wanted man this side of the Mississippi. There's a reward of two thousand dollars posted for his capture, dead or alive. Reckon most of you have heard of Ed Clayton.'

'Ed Clayton.' There were faint gasps of astonishment from the men assembled in the room. Dan would have been surprised if there hadn't been. Clayton was one of the most notorious men back east. Only he and Bateson knew that he was, at that very moment, safely in jail over five hundred miles away.

Outside, he stood quite still as two more men, seated in the saddle, held rifles trained on him. From the looks on their faces, he guessed that they thought he was none other than the notorious Ed Clayton and the knowledge gave him a little more confidence, the feeling that perhaps, after all, this plan might work.

Twenty minutes later, the stage arrived in front of the saloon. Dan was thrust unceremoniously inside while the sheriff and one of the men climbed in with him. Out of the corner of his eye, as he settled back into his seat, his hands chained together, Dan saw the heavy strong box being loaded on board. This time, they had taken the precaution of changing the contents at the very last minute and he felt certain that no one in Carson knew of this apart from Sheriff Bateson and himself. As far as everyone else was concerned, it contained over a dozen heavy gold bars and dollar bills. There was even a small number of genuine dollar bills on top of the useless cargo inside, just in case anyone did have the chance to open the box and take a quick look inside.

The driver whipped up the team and moments later, the coach was rattling and swaying along the main street, out of Carson and headed for Shannon City. Seated in the corner, Dan felt the tension in his body beginning to mount as the minutes ticked by with an agonising slowness. It anything had gone wrong, if there had been quite a small point which they had overlooked, it could mean a quick end for him. That was a risk he was quite prepared to take but he would have felt better facing it with a gun in his hand. He watched the country flow past them as the stage lurched forward, the driver occasionally touching the team with the whip to urge them on.

By the time they had reached the halfway point between Carson and Shannon City, he knew that the Carron gang would have to make their play within minutes or not at all. Still there seemed to be no sign of them as he had the sudden sinking feeling that in spite of all the precautions he and Bateson had taken to prevent anything of this leaking out, the gang had somehow got wind of it and did not intend to attack. Then, almost before he was aware of it, the sharp bark of a rifle bit through the beat of the horses' hooves and there was a sudden sharp lurch which almost caused the stage to turn over on its side as the driver pulled up the team. A bullet smashed through the woodwork close to Dan's head as the coach swayed on its leather braces on the uneven trail.

The man accompanying the sheriff suddenly leaned sideways, thrust his gun out of the window and began firing wildly along the trail. A few seconds later, he uttered a sharp cry and pulled his arm back into the coach. Blood was beginning to well from the bullet wound and he pawed frantically at it, trying to stem the flow of blood. A swift glance was enough to tell Dan that it was nothing but a flesh wound that looked more serious than it really was.

Jolted and bruised by the coach as it swung from side to side, Dan was forced to thrust himself far back into his seat, straightening his legs as he did so, to prevent himself from falling forward on to his face. There was the sound of voices from outside and the stage came to a halt at a sharp bend in the trail.

'Everyone get out of the coach,' yelled a harsh voice. 'And keep your hands where we can see them. Don't try to go for your guns, gentlemen, and no one will get hurt.'

Another gruff voice shouted up to the driver. 'Throw down that strongbox and hurry.'

As he stumbled from the coach, finding it difficult to

maintain his balance, Dan saw the strongbox being pitched from the buckboard. It landed with a dull thud in the dirt and two of the outlaws moved forward and picked it up, carrying it to the side of the trail. There, Dan knew, they would shoot off the lock and take a look at the contents and that was something he did not want them to do until he had said his piece.

He pushed himself forward, away from Sheriff Bateson's restraining hands. One of the men glanced down quickly, lowering the barrel of his gun. Then he seemed to relax abruptly. When he spoke there was a cultured note in his voice and Dan knew immediately, even though the man's face was masked, that this was Luke Carron. Once, the other had been a promising lawyer back east, but somehow, he had fallen in with his brother and now followed a life of crime.

'Well, and what have we here?' The eyes above the mask lifted towards the sheriff. 'One of your prisoners, Sheriff. Seems like this is his lucky day.' The gaze shifted to Dan. 'What's your name?'

Dan drew himself up to his full height and looked the other squarely in the eye. 'My name is Ed Clayton,' he said thinly. 'I can guess who you are, but it might be embarrassing at the moment if I were to say.'

'Clayton?' There was deep surprise in the other's voice. 'Sure I've heard of you. But how come you're so far west? And more to the point, where are these men taking you?'

'Into Shannon City,' said Dan thinly. 'They've got a trial all set on a murder charge. Seems somebody wanted that reward money so bad, they turned me in.'

The other leaned forward over the neck of his mount and addressed Sheriff Bateson. 'I reckon we'll have to relieve you of your prisoner, Sheriff,' he said mockingly. 'But it doesn't seem right to my way of thinking that you should go through with this trial against him. Could be that you'd decided to claim that reward money for yourself. If so, I'm afraid I'm going to disappoint you.'

'You'll never get sway with this, I promise you. I'll hunt

you down and run you to earth if it's the last thing I do.'

'Don't tempt me too far, Sheriff.' The steel was beginning to show through the almost lazy indifference in the other's voice. 'Now one of you gentlemen unlock those chains on Clayton's wrists. I see there are no more passengers and as I doubt whether either of you will be carrying any valuables, we won't bother to search you. Once you've set this man free, unhitch one of the horses from the team and leave him out. The others will be enough to get you into Shannon City.'

No one saw the flicker of relief which crossed Sheriff Bateson's face as he came close to Dan and unlocked the chains around his wrists, a look which said, more clearly than words, that the first part of their plan had been successfully accomplished and that now it was up to Dan to carry out the rest, that Bateson had given him all the help in his power. From that moment on, he was on his own.

'All right,' ordered Luke Carron as the Sheriff stepped back. 'Everyone into the coach. If anyone tries to follow us, he'll be dead before evening, I promise you.'

Dan knew that it was no idle threat as he stood by the side of the trail and watched as the two men climbed back inside the stage and the driver clambered into his seat. A few moments later, the coach was rumbling along the trail in the direction of Shannon City and Dan was clambering up into the saddle of the horse which had been cut out of the team.

'I don't know how to thank you,' he said hoarsely as he sat easily in the saddle. 'I expected to find myself on the end of a rope by tomorrow. This seems to have been my lucky day.'

'Save the thanks until later,' said the other brusquely, 'Let's get out of here while we can. Bring that strong box along with you, Jeb. We'll open it back at camp.'

'Are you taking this *hombre* back with us'?' asked Jeb thickly. He eyed Dan from over the top of his mask and there was undisguised hostility in his gaze. 'I don't take well to showing any strangers our camp. This could be a trap.'

'Talk sense, Jeb,' snarled the other. 'This here is Ed Clayton and you don't expect any man who faces a hanging session, to go and give himself up just to turn us in do you? Besides, he could be a very useful addition to the band.'

There were murmurs of assent from the other men. 'If he's as good with a gun as the stories say he is, then he'll be a handy man to have around,' grunted one of the men.

'I can handle a gun,' said Dan quietly. 'That's one of the reasons they wanted me in Shannon City. Somebody swore that it wasn't a fair fight although the two men drew before I did. Reckon they just wanted a charge they could make stick.'

'You'll do,' said Luke Carron. He swung his mount's head and put it into a gallop, leaving the trail behind and heading into the trees. The rest of the gang followed him, with Dan riding with them. Leaving the trees, they cut down into the desert and headed almost due south. There was a rising excitement inside Dan's mind and the muscles of his stomach had bunched themselves into a tight, almost painful, knot. Very soon. now, he told himself, he would discover the location of the Carron gang's hideout. Once he had done that, he would need to figure out some way of getting the information through to Sheriff Bateson without any of these men becoming suspicious.

CHAPTER TWO

HIDE-OUT

THEY rode out into the yellow, alkaline wilderness that was the desert, away from the trails, from the more frequented waterholes and the sand muffled the sound of their hard riding, while the sun lifted higher towards its zenith, beating down upon their heads and shoulders. Dan narrowed his eyes as he followed the others, trying to file away all of the landmarks into his brain, ready for the time when they might be needed again.

'Aren't you afraid that the sheriff might be trailing us?' he asked suddenly, glancing round at Luke Carron.

'He'd be a g'darned fool if he does.' There was no emotion in the other's voice. 'The desert is an evil place. If we don't kill him, the wilderness will. He won't be the first to try to trail us to our hide-out. There have been others.'

'And what happened to them?' asked Dan casually. There was a peculiar tightness in his body, but he was careful to allow none of it to show through into his voice.

'They're buzzard-meat by now.' No feeling in Luke's tone. For the first time, Dan realised just what kind of men these were. Murder and violence meant nothing to them. He wondered what would happen when they discovered that the strongbox, which Jeb Carron carried on the saddle in front of him, proved to contain nothing but stones and a handful of dollar bills.

Luke Carron eased his mount towards Dan's. He said: 'You could be a useful man if you decide to throw in your lot with us, Clayton. But I must admit I'm still a little curious about you. These aren't your stamping grounds. The last I heard of you, you were still operating down in Alabama. Why did you suddenly move here, several hundred miles to the west?'

Dan shrugged. 'I had the law on my tail back east and decided that it was time for me to seek new pastures. No sense in moving further east, so I lit out in this direction. I figured that the frontier towns, with smaller army garrisons, would be a better place for me; so here I am. Thanks to you, I'm still free, otherwise, I might be swinging on the end of a rope in Shannon City.'

Luke Carron clucked sympathetically. 'We all know what it is to have the law on our trail, Clayton. 'That's why I figure you're safe only so long as you stay with us. To my way of thinking, that's a good guarantee of our own safety.'

Dan's jaw set hard. 'Seems to me that you still don't trust me.'

'Shall we say that we have found it wise never to trust anyone, too much. So long as you throw in your lot with us. that's all right by me. But if you once step out of line, if you once try to double-cross us, then you'll die. Is that quite clear?'

Dan shrugged again. 'It seems that I'm still in your hands. You've saved my life and for that I'm grateful. But I may have my own plans. There are those in Shannon City I have business with, those who would have strung me up without any trial.'

Luke Carron laughed, a harsh travesty of mirth. 'Even we do not underestimate the sheriff of Shannon City and you would be a fool to do so. We confine our activities to the stretch of country between Shannon City and Carson. So far, it has proved to be very profitable. I assure you that if you set foot in either town, you'll be a dead man. There must be plenty of men hoping for that reward money and you can't fight all of them.'

Dan lapsed into silence and turned his attention to the country through which they were travelling. On their right, the long buttes stretched away into the desert, empty and shimmering in the afternoon heat. Overhead, a small flock of vultures wheeled in lazy circles against the brilliant, blue-white mirror of the sky. No wonder it had proved virtually impossible to discover where these men hid themselves after they had robbed the stages between Shannon City and Carson. Here, in the vast empty stillness of the desert, a man could lose himself for a hundred years, especially if he knew the multitude of trails which wound, almost unseen except to trained eyes, across the wilderness.

An hour later, Luke Carron called a halt at a small waterhole which lay in the middle of the desert; a place where a few stunted bushes grew around it in the arid earth. Dan slid thankfully out of the saddle, felt the heat of the desert striking through his boots. He glanced about him in surprise.

'This can't be your hide-out.' He drained the last drops from his water-bottle, wiped the back of his sleeve over his lips, then bent to fill it again.

'You're right, Clayton, it isn't.' There was a sharpness to Jeb Carron's tone. He eased his guns in and out of their holsters with a deliberate movement. 'The hide-out is still several miles from here. You'll get there in good time.'

Dan nodded. It would be unwise to ask too many questions at the moment. Looking from one to the other, he wondered which of the two brothers was the more dangerous. Jeb looked the killer-type, ready and eager to use his guns. But even so, there was something about Luke which made him pause. Behind that suave and seemingly indifferent exterior, he had the impression there was a smouldering hatred for anything concerned with the law; something to do with the other's past, he guessed. No, he reflected, Jeb was the kind of man he was used to handling. Luke, on the other hand, would bear watching.

He was aware that Luke was eyeing him curiously. The

other was still not completely satisfied with the answers he had been given. But he knew that the other would bide his time, watch him closely for the first wrong move which would say that he wasn't Clayton, knowing that when that happened, he would still have the whip hand.

Two of the men started a fire with some sage-brush they had gathered and they squatted around the waterhole; eating beans and bacon. The sun continued to lower towards the west and the hot wind was now smothering, blowing out of the south, beginning to pick up dust which worked its way into the sweat-soaked folds of their flesh, itching and irritating. Dan tried to visualize what Sheriff Bateson would be doing now. He had insisted that the other should not try to follow them, knowing that the gang would be expecting something like this and it could lead to nothing but trouble. Far better that he should go it alone, try to discover everything he could about these outlaws and then, somehow, figure a way of getting the information back to Shannon City, either in person, or by leaving a message somewhere where it could be found. There would doubtless come a time in the near future when these men would ride out again on another raid. Either they would take him with them or, if Luke Carron was still suspicious, they would leave him at their camp with possibly a couple of men to keep a watch over him. Already, his agile mind was thinking ahead, scheming, trying to figure out some way in which he could pass on anything he learned to Bateson.

The outlaws seemed to take their time at the waterhole. He had expected them to be on their way as soon as they had finished their meal, but instead they took their time, and before they climbed back into the saddles, Jeb Carron looked over at his brother and said harshly: 'What say we take a look inside this durned strong box, Luke? Ain't no sense in carrying all that weight with us when we could blow off the lock here and just take what's inside. The box ain't no use to us.'

There were grunts of assent from the others gathered

31

around the waterhole. Dan saw Luke nod slowly and a moment later, Jeb rose to his feet, untied the thick rope which bound it to his saddle and let it fall with a dull thump to the ground. The sharp crash of the gun shot was lost almost instantly in the desert and only the slowly wheeling vultures gave any indication of noticing it.

Bending, Jeb threw back the lid of the box, delved inside, pulling out the dollar bills which had been laid neatly on top, then uttered a sharp curse.

'We've been tricked, Luke. There ain't nothin' in here but sand and stones. A handful of dollar bills on top to make it look good.' He spun on Luke. 'I thought you said this had been checked by—' He broke off suddenly and threw a quick glance at Dan from beneath lowered lids.

Luke strode forward quickly, stood looking down into the open box, then swung on Dan. 'Do you know anything about this, Clayton?' he demanded thinly.

Dan was aware of the accusing eyes of the rest of the outlaws fixed on him, watching his face for the faintest sign of emotion. He shook his head in dull surprise. 'I heard them say they'd take the strong box through to Shannon City, but that was all.' He shrugged. 'From the way they were handling it and keeping the news secret, I figured there was something mighty valuable inside it.'

'Well, there ain't,' snarled Jeb Carron brusquely. 'Looks to me as if the sheriff knew that stage was going to be held up.'

'Or your information was wrong.' Dan realized instantly, that in order to divert suspicion from himself, he would have to try a big bluff. He whirled on Luke Carron. 'Evidently you've been getting information from someone inside Carson, who's been tipping you off as to the cargo carried by the stages. Seems he's been double-crossing you. Probably wants a bigger cut for himself, or maybe even thinks he's better off alone.'

'You seem to know quite a lot, Clayton,' snapped Jeb, without waiting for his brother to answer. 'Far too much for somebody who's just been in the territory for a little while.'

'Don't be a fool,' said Dan heatedly. 'Anyone can see how you've been operating. I've used the same style myself back in Dodge. Only I made sure that he didn't double-cross me. If he's got access to that strongbox so's he can tell you beforehand what's in it, then he could just as easily have taken out that gold you expected to find, and stached it away for himself.'

A wary look came into Jeb's eyes and his thin lips tight-ened, into a hard line across his face. 'If I thought that—'

'Quiet, Jeb,' interrupted Luke. He rummaged inside the strongbox for a moment, then rose lithely to his feet, his dark, handsome face taut with anger and concentra-tion. 'There's more to this than just a case of us being double-crossed. Things aren't adding up at all.' He picked up the dollar bills lying on the ground and stuffed them inside his shirt. 'Tomorrow, you'll ride into Carson, Jeb, and ferret things out for yourself. And the answers you get had better he good.'

There was an ominous note to his voice which boded ill for their informant if he failed to satisfy Jeb. Dan saddled up as the others moved towards their mounts. For the moment, it seemed he had successfully diverted suspicion from himself and placed it on the unknown informant. But once Jeb Carron rode into Carson it would soon become apparent that this man, whoever he was, had had nothing to do with the exchange of the strongbox contents and the suspicion towards him would grow again. It was a pity he could not find any excuse for riding into Carson with Jeb. That way, he might be able to kill two birds with one stone. Discover the identity of the man supplying this very valuable information and possibly get word throuh to Bateson.

When the others had hit leather, they rode almost due west for the best part of fifteen miles, heading towards the range of low hills which bordered the desert in that direc-tion. As they drew closer, Dan saw that the slopes of the hills were covered with stunted bushes and that high up, on the crests of the long, low ridges, there were tall pines.

33

This was new country to him. He had not probed as far south or west as this when he had ridden into Shannon City, but his frontier sense had stood him in good stead and he felt reasonably confident that he would be able to find his own way back to the main trail and also back here if the opportunity ever came.

Dan stared at the hills as they drew closer, leaning forward over the pommel of the saddle. 'Looks to me as if you've picked yourselves a mighty fine hiding place,' he said soberly. 'If there's desert on the other side of those hills, as I reckon there is, you'd be able to stand off an army, let alone a sheriff's posse. And out here in the middle of the desert, you'll be able to spot anyone approaching for miles.'

One of the men grinned hugely. 'They've never been able to find us so far,' he said gruffly. 'But they never give up trying. Seems like everybody in the territory wants to get their hands on that reward money."

'Don't forget there's a couple of thousand dollars on my head too – dead or alive,' muttered Dan. 'But before they take me, there are a few old scores I have to settle in Shannon City.'

Luke Carron threw him a sidelong glance. 'You ain't thinking of going back there,' he said sharply. 'Not after what happened in Carson. Every sheriff and deputy in the territory will be on the look out for you.'

The note in the other's tone was sufficient to warn Dan that the other's words were not said out of concern for him, but rather as a warning to him not to try to slip off on his own.

'Mebbe so,' he said easily, ignoring the edge in Luke's tone. 'But there are one or two things in every man's past that he can't forget, that count above everything else. Things he has to do before he dies.'

'Go on,' prompted the other. 'What sort of things?'

'That sheriff who was taking me in to Shannon City. His name is Bateson. He was back east when I first ran into him. A fast man with a gun, but I guess he was no match for me. I killed one of his deputies, in fair fight, tried to shoot me in the back in one of the saloons in Dodge. He swore he'd get me.'

'Obviously he didn't,' said Luke Carron grimly.

'No.' Dan forced bitterness into his tone. 'He come after me. Somebody tipped him off where to find me. Fortunately, I wasn't there when he surrounded the place with a posse. But he caught my kid brother, trussed him up and took him back into Dodge. There wasn't anything they could pin on him; only the fact that he had been hiding me until there was a chance for me to skip out of the territory.

'But he couldn't get his hands on me, so he did the one thing he knew would hurt me. He trumped up a couple of charges against my kid brother, brought him before a judge who happened to be a particular friend of his and had a guilty verdict brought in against him. They hung him the next day, right there in the middle of Dodge. I swore then that I'd hunt him down and kill him for the dirty coyote that he is.'

Luke Carron grinned. 'Seems to me that if we hadn't held up that stage this afternoon, they'd have hung you too.'

Dan nodded his head slowly. 'Could be. But I'm still alive and the next time, he'll be on the wrong end of a gun.'

'You'll have to bide your time, Clayton.' There was no emotion in the flat voice. 'As far as we're concerned, you know just a little too much. You ride with us, or you stay here with two men to guard you, the choice is yours.'

Dan made as if to protest, then shrugged his shoulders in resignation. 'I don't seem to have any choice,' he said softly. 'But you aren't aiming to keep me a prisoner, are you?'

'Only until we're satisfied about you,' said the other smoothly. 'You see our position. We can't afford to make any mistakes. We're alive now, because we don't take any chances. We intend to keep it that way.'

They reached the edge of the desert and in front of

35

them, a narrow trail wound up the lower slopes of the hills, vanishing as it entered the thick trees at the crest. Jeb led the way, easing his mount forward, the others following in single file, with Dan riding directly in front of Luke who brought up the rear. The trail wound in and out of patches of open ground, dotted here and there by huge boulders. At the top, as they entered the shade of the tall trees, Dan felt the sudden coolness on his heated body and there was the crisp smell of the pines in his nostrils, going down like wine into his lungs. He took deep breaths of it as he followed the others, eyes flicking swiftly from side to side. Over the crest, they wound their way downward again, reaching the bottom of the hill on the far side. In front of them, there was desert again, and for a moment, Dan thought that he had made a mistake, that they still had several miles to go across that harsh, alkali waste. Then, abruptly, Jeb wheeled his mount sharply to the right, along a narrow trail that ran parallel with the base of the hills. Several moments passed before Dan saw the wide mouth of the cave which ran back into the hill itself. Until one was right on top of it, it would have been virtually impossible to see it. The opening was cunningly camouflaged with branches and bracken and as he ducked his head and rode inside, he was forced to admire the ingenuity of these men for although the cave itself was clearly a natural formation, the camouflaging of it had been their own work.

'You'll be quite safe from the law here,' said Luke, sliding down from the saddle. 'Make yourself at home. We've enough food and water stached away here to withstand any siege . . . . That's one big advantage of being holed up in the middle of the desert. Your pursuers have got to pull back for food first. They can't hope to sit tight and starve us out.'

Dan nodded to himself as he dropped easily to the ground and stared about him, For the first time, he realized the almost absolute impregnability of this position. From the top of the wooded crest, it would be possible for one man to watch in both directions and see anyone approaching over the desert almost an hour before they would be able to get there, even pushing their mounts to the limit. By that time, the whole of the gang would be holed up, ready to stave off any attack. He tightened his lips thinly. It would need an army of law officers to prise these men out of their hide-out, even if they managed to find it, and in that tremendous wilderness of heat and sun-blistered sand, that was going to be a difficult problem.

Inside the cave, he found that it stretched back into the hillside in a series of tunnels and guessed that, at one time in the past, it had probably been one of the old mines which had been worked in the area, and which, having been worked out, had been abandoned and possibly forgotten for many years. Somehow, these outlaws must have stumbled upon it and seen the possibilities at once. He felt a grudging admiration for the way in which they had fitted it out. The surroundings were austere, but there was furniture of a sort. Piles of skins in one corner clearly served as beds for them and there was a couple of tables and several chairs, possibly looted from one of the nearby towns. On a stone ledge, he noticed the pile of tins and going forward, found that they contained beans and meat, enough to last for several weeks. Luke Carron had not been exaggerating when he had claimed that they had sufficient food to withstand any siege which the law could bring to bear on them.

Already, his quick brain was thinking ahead, trying to figure out any means by which these men could be destroyed. It was obvious that, even if he managed to get back in Shannon City, give Sheriff Bateson the location of these outlaws and their hide-out, it would not be enough. Either they would have to take these men by surprise – and on the face of it that did not seem likely – or they would have to attack when the majority of the outlaws were away, be ready for them when they returned.

'Well, Clayton, what do you think of our little hide-out?' Jeb Carron turned and grinned at him, the lips

37

twisted into what seemed to be an almost perpetual sneer. 'Sometimes, I get to wishing that the law really did find this place. I reckon we could show 'em just how strongly fortified it is.'

Dan nodded. 'You figure they ever will find it?' he asked easily.

'Not a chance.' Luke stamped into the cave, sat down at the table. 'You saw for yourself that there are no trails leading in this direction. They'd have to stumble on the place by accident as we did.'

'I figured that was how you must have located it.' He jerked his thumb in the direction of the dark tunnels which led into the back of the cave. 'Where do they lead to? A dead end?'

The other shook his head and there was a faint smile on his face. 'Just in case anyone does find us and manages to get past our defences. There's a way through there out into the desert about two miles from here.'

'But you have to know just which tunnel to take and where to turn, Clayton,' muttered Jeb. 'If you lose your way back there, you'll wander through those tunnels for an eternity before anybody finds you.'

'I'm just beginning to realize how strong a position you have here,' he admitted. 'If only there were a place like this back at Dodge, I could have given that posse a run for their money and still have been there.'

Jeb gave a sharp guffaw. 'I reckon you can see now, why it would be worth your while to throw in your lot with us, Clayton. We're sitting on top of everything here'

'I guess you're right,' said Dan slowly. He rubbed his chin thoughtfully. 'And assuming that I do, what's in it for me?'

'Now you're talking,' said Luke. 'The way we work at the moment, equal shares for every man. An eighth for you, the same as for everybody else.'

'Sounds fair enough.'

'OK, then, that's settled.' The other got to his feet. 'We'll be ready to move in on another stage in about three days. You've probably guessed by now that we take very few chances. We have an agent in Carson who tips us off when there's something worth taking on the stage.'

'Seems he wasn't right today,' Dan inclined his head towards the small pile of bills on the table in front of Luke.

'Don't worry, We'll look into that. If we are being double-crossed there'll be retribution.'

He left it there but Dan guessed that retribution would be swift and sure. There was something at the back of the other's tone which sent a little shiver of apprehension through him.

That night, as he lay beneath the pile of skins, the musty smell irritating the back of his nostrils, his mind was casting ahead, trying to figure a way out of this situation, a way in which he could get word through to Bateson, or at a pinch, to get away from the gang now that he knew everything he wanted,

Two mornings later, one of the gang rode off to the north-west. Dan stood in the opening of the cave and watched him climb the trail through the trees on top of the ridge until he vanished from sight. Turning, he found Luke Carron watching him closely, with that same speculative look in his eyes. 'Clem will be back by nightfall. When he returns, we'll know which stage to hold up. Then we'll see if you're as handy with a gun as the legends say you are.' He nodded towards the guns in Dan's holsters, guns which had belonged to some man they had killed in the past, someone who would no longer be needing them. Dan had checked that they were loaded. The mechanism of both worked with a buttered smoothness and they were accurately balanced.

'To me,' went on Luke smoothly, 'a gun is like a woman. Beautiful, but deadly. Don't you think so, Clayton?'

'I wouldn't know,' shrugged Dan. 'I ain't got any use for women. And as for guns, I guess they can get a man into trouble unless he knows how to handle them.'

'If you stick with us, Clayton, you'll find that life is full of trouble. The strong man welcomes it because it is something he can face up to and overcome. The coward runs away from it. However, I'm quite sure that you've never run away from trouble in your life.'

Dan gave a quick nod. 'No reason why I should. Back in Dodge, you lived only as long as you could outdraw the law officers who were determined to take you, dead or alive.'

Luke said very softly: 'I'm still trying to figure you, Clayton. Some things about you that don't quite add up, Don't get me wrong, just that we can't afford to take any chances. There's a rope somewhere with your name on it. OK be that as it may, I assure you it means nothing to us. Me, I don't care a damn whether you killed all of those men back in Dodge or not. So long as you stick by us, I'll be quite content. But the one thing I do demand from everyone in the outfit, is absolute loyalty.'

In spite of the smoothness in the other's tone, Dan recognized the sinister note at the back of the smoothness. The other was telling him, in no uncertain terms, that he would be watched until they were absolutely sure of him. That the first wrong move he made would be his last. He did not doubt that these men would shoot him in the back if he made any move which could be construed as disloyalty to the gang.

When the man returned, shortly before nightfall, they gathered inside the cave, Dan standing in the background eyeing the others from beneath lowered lids. Luke, seated at the table, with Jeb standing at his right hand, said to the man: 'What did you find in Carson, Clem? Did you check on that matter of the strongbox?'

The other nodded, leaned forward, resting his hands on the table in front of Luke. 'There's something mighty funny about that, boss. There's no doubt that the gold and dollar bills were in that box when it left the Wells Fargo office. Seems that somebody must have switched it on the way to the stage point.'

Luke's brows knit in sudden thought. 'So, that means the sheriff must have been in on the deal. He's the only one who could have had access to that box, who could have switched the contents without being noticed. He must have suspected that the stage would be held up.'

'Has this ever happened before?' asked Dan, speaking up.

'Once,' admitted the other. 'But there's no need to worry, Clayton. It isn't going to happen again, we've already seen to that.'

Dan nodded, showing that he was satisfied with the answer. He wondered what had happened back in Carson to make the other so sure, then pushed the thought into the background of his mind as Luke went on: 'When are they sending the next shipment of gold through to Shannon City?'

'Day after tomorrow. No doubt about it this time. It'll be a big shipment, and they'll have guards escorting the stage. Probably they might even station some along the trail to be on the safe side.' He grinned viciously. 'Seems we've got 'em worried back there in Carson, boss.'

'Mebbe so. I don't like that idea of men posted along the trail. It means we'll have to check the whole stretch where we're going to attack.' He paused and ran a finger reflectively along his cheek. 'But that isn't an insurmountable obstacle. We've done it before. Two men will scout the trail for any guards. If they find any, I want them killed with the minimum of trouble and fuss.' He looked over two of the men near the back of the cave. 'Gomez and Carlos. You can carry out that part of the plan. Quick and silent. You understand?'

The two men, their high cheek bones testifying to their Mexican ancestry even more so than their names, gave quick nods and fingered the long-bladed knives in their belts.

'What about the rest of us, Luke?' asked Dan quietly, He deliberately kept all emotion out of his tone. The thought of the cold-blooded way in which the other intended to kill any men guarding the trail sent a quiver of anger coursing through his body.

'I'm coming to that.' The other refused to be hurried.

'We'll take the stage at the fork in the trail six miles outside of Carson. There's plenty of cover there and we can be upon them before they know where we are. We'll shoot down the escort from cover, then close in.'

To Dan, that sounded like murder, pure and simple; but at the moment, he could see no way of preventing it. If he showed his hand prematurely, it would mean the end of him. He would have to choose his time carefully if he was to stand any chance of survival at all.

Quietly, Luke Carron outlined the plan of campaign for attacking the stage. It was quite clear that the other had fought in the war, had been a man accustomed to giving orders, who knew how to plan actions. The military precision with which he had planned this action showed through quite clearly.

The sun was high in a cloudless blue sky when they rode out of the cave, up through the trees and down the side of the steep slope, out into the stretching desert which lay beyond. Their water bottles were filled to the brim and they rode fast with the sun, several degrees up from the horizon, shining brilliantly down at them, with the promise of heat to come. Dan made a mental note of the landmarks as they rode, past the deep waterhole where they had rested up a few days before, then almost due north, towards the dark smudge on the horizon which indicated the position of the main trail from Carson to Shannon City.

Dan had still found no solution to the problems which were striking deep at his mind, growing more and more urgent as the minutes passed. It would be impossible for him to warn those men who might be watching the trail, to warn them that within an hour at the most, two silent and vicious killers would be moving in on them, to strike and kill without sound, without a chance for them to defend themselves. He had no doubt that Gomez and Carlos had done this sort of thing many times before. They were old hands at the game and none of the deputies which Bateson could swear in would stand a chance against them.

42

He himself had lived too long with danger and death, not to be able to visualise with a sharp clarity what would happen, unless he could do something about it. The sun climbed to its zenith and then began to descend slowly. They rode without pause, occasionally drinking from their water bottles to wash down the yellow alkaline dust which clogged their mouths and throats. Their mounts began to flag a little as they reached the edge of the desert. They had been riding hard for close on four hours, across some of the most terrible country in the territory.

A quarter of a mile from the rough, rocky ground which marked the edge of the trail, Gomez and Carlos moved off, away from the main body, and rode in opposite directions. They would scout the trail, on both sides, for a distance of two or three miles in either direction, killing any man they found. By the time the rest of them attacked the stage, those escorting it would find that there would be no help coming from the others.

The minutes dragged on. They entered the coolness under the trees. Less than three hundred yards to the north lay the rocky trail along which the stage from Carson would come. If their information had been correct, there would be a fortune in gold in that strongbox and even if there were a dozen guards with the stage, at least half of them could be shot down from cover before they knew what was happening, especially if they were depending on their guards, posted at intervals along the trail, to warn them of any danger.

Dismounting at a point overlooking the fork, they crawled forward through the rough underbrush, out on to the rocks which rose ten to twelve feet above the trail itself. Cautiously, Dan lifted his head and stared in both directions.

Jeb struck a match and lit a cigarette, then stubbed it out quickly as his brother snapped harshly, his voice like the hissing of a snake. 'Put that out, Jeb. That smoke could be seen for miles, like an Indian signal, Do you want to give them warning that we're here?'

43

'G'darn it, Luke. They ain't within miles of here right now.' The other narrowed his eyes and stared along the empty trail. Not even a speck of dust spoiled the stillness where it wound between the rocks and a deep silence seemed to lie like a blanket over everything as the terrain drowsed in the heat of the early afternoon.

Dan sucked in his lips, screwing up his eyes to reduce the glare of the sunlight. Luke Carron had chosen this place well. From the cover of the rocks, it would be possible for them to pour a concentrated and withering hail of fire into the stage and any riders accompanying it, without exposing themselves to any return fire. And if the driver tried to whip up the team, the minute he heard the first shot, he would merely drive them towards the rocks in which they lay hidden.

Any attempt to turn the coach at the fork would expose it to the full blast of gunfire, would provide the minimum of cover for the men riding in it.

'How long do you figure it'll be before they get here?' muttered Jeb. He chewed on a plug of tobacco.

'If they're on time, another twenty minutes,' acknowledged Luke. 'Time we got some men to the far side of the trail. Jeb, take Clem and Clayton here with you. Wait for our shots before you open fire. I don't want this thing going off half-cock.'

Dan followed Jeb and Clem down the slope, across the trail, and into the rocks on the other side. Here they settled down, scanning the trail for the first sign of the stage. Dan waited in cool expectancy, outwardly calm, but inwardly his brain was a raging turmoil. It was possible that Bateson was riding with the escort, maybe expecting trouble, and perhaps relying on him to help. He said to Jeb: 'Don't you reckon this is a mighty dangerous position for us, Jeb?'

The other looked at him sharply. 'What's gotten into you, Clayton? Getting scared all at once'?'

'Now, you know that ain't true,' he protested hotly. 'But if I'm to fight for an equal share of the takings, I'd like to

44

think that I'm taking an equal share of the risks, no more and no less.'

'Just what are you getting at?' The other's eyes narrowed slightly, the lips twisted back into an interrogative sneer.

'Just this. We know there's a big escort riding with this stage and it's more than likely that we won't be able to shoot them all down at once, before they hit dirt and get under cover.'

'So we go in and finish them off from both sides,' growled the other harshly. 'What's wrong with that? Or do you prefer to do your fighting from a distance where you won't get hurt.'

'Careful what you're saying Jeb,' he warned. 'Mebbe your brother does run this outfit, but I don't take insults from you or anybody else. Just remember that. But I've been watching you lately. Luke may be your brother, but you're the better man. You ought to be head of this outfit – and I figure that a lot of the men think the same way.'

A look of surprise passed momentarily over the other's coarse features and Dan knew that his remark had struck home. He pressed on with the temporary advantage, knowing that he had to work fast, that now the seed of suspicion had been sown in the other's mind, he had to crystallize it into something more than that – and time was running out swiftly. At any moment, they might hear the thunder of approaching hooves and see the cloud of dust which would mark the position of the stage.

'I reckon that Luke has noticed this too, Jeb,' he went on softly, his voice quiet and persuasive. 'That's why he sent you over here with Clem and me. He knows that if things do go wrong with this attack, if there are too many of them for us to handle, we're cut off. Our horses are over on the other side of the trail, Jeb. To get to them we'll have to run the gauntlet of their fire and some, if not all of us, are going to get killed in the process. Besides, it would be the simplest thing of all for him to stampede our horses when he pulls out, or take them with him.'

'You know, I ought to shoot you for saying anything like that, Clayton,' snarled the other, lips drawn back, showing the uneven teeth.

'Then why don't you?' asked Dan quietly. 'Shall I tell you? It isn't because you need me as an extra gun to help you shoot down these deputies. It's because you know I'm right. Luke hates your guts, just as much as you hate his. With a man like you running this outfit, a mistake like that which happened with the last stage, wouldn't have occurred.'

Dan could see that the other was struggling within himself, thinking this thing out. 'With all of the gold that he gets from this hold-up, he could be set up for life,' he persisted. 'Once he's over the Mexican border, he'll be safe. But he won't include you in his plans, or Clem, or myself.'

Jeb turned swiftly towards Clem and motioned him forward. The other crawled over to them; 'Yeah?'

'The gold that they're carrying on this stage. Did you find out how much there is?"

'Sure. Close on three hundred thousand dollars' worth. Then there's the dollar bills. Couldn't rightly say how many of them there are,'

Jeb grunted. 'Could be that you're right,' he muttered. 'I hadn't figured on as much as that. What do you reckon we ought to do?'

'That's easy. One of us has to get across to our horses and lead them over here, before the stage shows up and without being seen.'

'And how do I know I can trust you, Clayton?'

'You don't. Only I'm here with you and it was Luke's idea for us to come this side, not mine.'

The other hesitated, then nodded. He turned to Clem. 'You heard what he said. Keep under cover, head down the trail a piece, then cut over, behind them and bring our horses back this side. They'll be too busy watching for the stage to see you.' As an afterthought, he added: 'And keep a sharp look out for Gomez and

46

Carlos. They may shoot you in mistake for one of the lawmen.'

For a moment, Dan thought that the other meant to protest, but after a second he gave a brief nod and slithered away among the rocks, his head well down.

Now that he was alone with Jeb, Dan's thoughts began to crystallize inside his mind. He had only one man to take care of and if he had planned things well, it meant that Clem would he unable to get back across the trail until the stage was in sight. Gently, he eased the gun from its holster, held it ready in the palm of his hand, fingers curled tightly around the barrel. He did not dare to risk a shot for that would have warned the outlaws on the other side of the trail. When the time came, he would have to dispose of Jeb quickly and silently. Out of the corner of his eye, he caught sight of Clem, a few moments later, moving across the trail, about a hundred yards further along. From that position, it was extremely unlikely that any of the men on the far side would be able to see him, and a few seconds later, the dark, hunched figure slithered out of sight among the rocks on the opposite bank of the trail. He let out his breath slowly and quietly. The first part of his plan had been successfully accomplished. He was under no illusions about Jeb Carron. The other was still suspicious of him, had not completely swallowed the tale he had tried to pitch him concerning his brother, but there had evidently been something brewing between the two of them for some time, otherwise it would not have been so easy to implant the seed of suspicion in Jeb's mind; clearly it had fallen upon fertile ground.

Everything now depended on the stage being on schedule, getting there before Clem succeeded in finding their horses, untethering them quietly and bringing them back across the trail. The other would undoubtedly be cautious, not wanting to give any indication to Luke. There would be swift and sure retribution if the other discovered what was happening.

'Looks like the stage now,' said Dan quietly. He pointed with his free hand to where a small patch of dust, no bigger than a man's hand had appeared along the trail in the direction of Carson. He heard Jeb suck in his breath sharply, then turn his head to glance along the trail in the opposite direction, obviously looking for Clem and the horses.

'Why doesn't Clem show himself?' snarled the other viciously, 'He's had plenty of time to get those mounts and bring them back. You think he might have warned Luke?'

'Could be.' Dan narrowed his eyes speculatively. 'It's something I hadn't figured on. If he has, then we're both finished.'

The other gave a quick grunt, then crawled forward, among the rocks, his gun in his hand, his face tight. Dan threw a swift glance along the trail, estimated that the stage would be there within two or three minutes and knew that the time had come for instant action. Swiftly, keeping his head down so that his actions could not be seen by the others across the trail, he went after Jeb. Even as he closed on him from behind, some sixth sense seemed to warn the outlaw that there was danger nearby, for he paused and turned his head sharply, jerking it around to stare at Dan as he went in with the gun upraised like a club.

The other's eyes widened momentarily and the hand holding the gun streaked up, the finger white with pressure on the trigger, trying to throw himself to one side even as Dan moved in.

With the speed of a striking rattler, Dan brought the butt of the gun crashing down, putting the whole of his wiry weight behind the blow. But the other was turning even as the gun fell and the butt caught him merely a glancing blow on the side of the temple, not sufficient to knock him cold completely, but enough to stun him slightly, to slow his movement, and to force him to relase his grip on the gun. It clattered to the rocks and went sliding down the slope on to the trail. Dan watched it fall with only a part of his attention. If any of the others had seen that sudden movement, there might be hell to pay. Even now, it was possible for his plans to be upset by the others. But there was no movement from the far rocks and even as Jeb was struggling to get to his feet, shaking his head dazedly, muttering a gruff curse under his breath, Dan swung again with the gun, making no mistake this time. The heavy steel butt crashed into the other's skull just behind the right ear. He uttered a low cough and collapsed on to the rocks, arms outflung, his legs twisted beneath him.

Dan paused only to make certain that he was either dead or deeply unconscious, then moved swiftly, further along the edge of the trail, until he reached a point almost directly opposite the fork in the trail. By now, the stage was so close that through the cloud of dust thrown up by the pounding hooves of the team, he was able to make out the half dozen men who rode with it, three on each side, grim and reliant men, their hands resting close to the guns at their waists.

He twisted his lips into a grim smile. Efficient as they were, they made excellent targets for Luke and his men crouched among the rocks. Well aimed shots could cut down more than half of them before they had a chance to go for their guns. Crouching down low, he eased the gun from its holster again, raised it carefully and snapped a quick shot at the leading rider. The bullet struck the dirt a couple of feet in front of the man's mount, kicking up a spurt of dust.

As a warning, it was more than sufficient. The driver of the stage reined the team to a halt, pulling on the hand brake. The escort slid off their horses and went to ground, their guns out. From just behind him, and on the far side of the trail, the outlaws opened up with every gun they had, but they had lost the element of surprise now. The escort were ready for them. Bullets thudded among the rocks close to Dan's head as he wriggled forward, snaking between huge boulders, hoping to get close enough to identify himself, before someone got lucky and hit him with a snap shot.

CHAPTER THREE

THE TRAP IS LAID

WITH the stealth of an Indian scout, Dan eased his way along the rocky rim of the terrain overlooking the trail until he was level with the stage and the men crouched down beside it. He saw too, that there were no ordinary passengers inside it, but armed men and one of them was, as he had suspected, Sheriff Bateson. There was another thick-set man with him whom he guessed to be the sheriff from Carson. Obviously with all that gold on board, they were determined to take no chances with the Carron gang.

Dan paused several times, alert and prepared, before he moved on. By the time he had reached a point among the rocks less than ten yards from the stage, the escort and the men inside had located the outlaws in their main position a little further along the trail and were firing systematically into the rocks. They were, however, making little impression on Luke and his men apart from forcing them to keep their heads well hidden.

Without the slightest whisper of sound, Dan moved forward until he lay on the very edge of the trail with only a single rock between him and the posse of lawmen. Harshly, he called: 'Bateson. Hold your fire. This is Dan Trafford. I'm coming in now.'

A pause, and then Bateson's voice reached him, just

loud enough for him to pick out the words. 'OK Dan. We're waiting for you.'

Swiftly, he crawled out of his hiding place, darted over to the stage and clambered inside. Bateson gave him a wide grin. 'I figured you were in on this deal, somewhere, Dan. Only you could have fired that warning shot. But we had to be sure. How many are there out there?'

'The whole gang. They've got two men ranging along the trail, with orders to knife any guards you've got posted. Jeb Saunders is unconscious about fifty yards away – mebbe dead. I hit him pretty hard. The others are on the far side of the trail among those rocks. You'll never hit them from here, they're under cover.'

'What do you figure we ought to do then?' asked the other man with the star pinned on his shirt. 'Can we work our way around 'em?'

'You might, but it'll take too long. They have their horses tethered back there in the trees ready for a quick get-away.'

The other pursed his lips. 'We planned this operation to net that gang,' he said harshly. 'Now that we have them on the wrong foot, I reckon we ought to step in and finish them off. It may be the only chance we'll get and by God, I figure we ought to take it.'

'It isn't going to be easy. You'll lose most of your men if you try to rush them. Your best plan would be to get some of your men mounted up and ride along the Tucson trail, try to get in behind them. You'll have to hit them before they ride out into the desert, or you'll lose them for good.'

The sheriff looked at him calmly, then gave a quick nod. Leaning from the window of the stage he issued orders to the men crouched down among the rocks nearby. A moment later, four of them were mounted and spurring their horses along the nearby trail. Perhaps, thought Dan, it was a forlorn hope. The volume of fire from the outlaw position had dwindled appreciably in the past minute or so while he had been talking. Clearly Luke had seen that the position was now hopeless, that he stood no chance of getting that strongbox without losing most of his men and had decided to pull out as quickly as he could, possibly recognizing it as a trap.

A few seconds later, the sound of horses being ridden away from the direction of the trees, reached their ears. Swiftly, Dan jumped from the stage, threw a quick glance along the trail. 'I figure you've lost them, Sheriff,' he said tightly, 'unless your men can ride faster than I think. Those outlaws know every trail in this territory and once in that desert, they'll soon shake off your men. But at least, everything isn't lost.'

'We still have the strongbox, if that's what you mean,' said Bateson and there was a trace of bitter disappointment in his voice. It was almost, thought Dan, as if he would willingly have lost that strongbox if, in return, they had killed most of the Carron gang.

'We may have something more than that,' Dan commented, moving forward quickly. 'We may have Jeb Carron. With him in our hands, it's just possible that his brother will come looking for him.'

He made his way into the rocks where he had left the unconscious form of Jeb Carron. There was the possibility that Clem had managed to get the horses and had found the other's body. During the commotion of the fighting, he could have thrown him over the saddle of one of the horses and ridden off with him. On the other hand Clem might have been too busy trying to save his own skin to worry about anyone else.

Jeb Carron was still where he had left him, lying among the rocks. Bending, Dan saw that he was still breathing and slipping the outlaw's second gun from its holster, he sent it spinning over the rocks into the trail. Bateson came up to him and stood for a moment staring down at Jeb Carron.

'At least we won't go back empty-handed,' he said with a sigh of relief. 'I'll get a couple of men to put him into the stage and we'll take him on into Shannon City. Once he's safely locked away in the jail there, I'll feel better. We can question him later.'

'If you can get him to talk,' said Dan grimly, 'Somehow, I think you'll find that difficult, even though I have managed to plant a seed of suspicion in his mind that his brother is trying to double-cross him.'

'I don't suppose there's much he can tell us that you don't know already, Dan,' said the other, looking up. 'You've been with them for some days now. You must know where they're hiding out.'

Dan nodded. 'It isn't going to be all that easy. I know where their hideout is and I reckon I could lead you to it. But you'd be spotted before you got to within five miles of it and the place is so well defended you'd need an army of men to get them out.'

'I had it figured for something like that,' admitted the other. 'You got any ideas at all about how we might go about this, Dan?'

'Some. But they'll all need careful thinking out. I reckon we ought to ride on into Shannon City and talk there. Your men won't be long in making their way back when they find that they can't follow Carron and his men into the desert.'

He climbed into the stage and seated himself opposite the two men who sat one on either side of the unconscious figure of Jeb Carron. There was an ugly purple bruise just on the other's temple where his first blow had hit him and a smear of blood on the side of his face. His breathing was harsh and rasping, his head lolling forward on to his chest as the stage started forward.

Swaying on its leather braces, the coach rattled along the uneven trail between the tall pines which blotted out much of the glaring sunlight, until they drove into the main street of Shannon City. Here, Jeb Carron, who had recovered consciousness was taken over to the jailhouse while Dan went with the sheriff into the small office overlooking the street, The rest of the men gathered around as he began to outline his plan for capturing the remainder of the dreaded Carron gang.

Sheriff Bateson had brought out a map of the surrounding territory which, as Dan had expected, showed the positions of the old gold and silver mines which had been filed and worked since the war. He pointed to one far out in the desert to the south-west of Shannon City.

'This is where they're holed up,' he said thinly. 'The old working here provides them with an excellent hide-out and they've got enough food, water and ammunition to withstand a long siege. We can't make a frontal attack. We'd be shot to pieces if we tried that. And there's no other way into the cave except through a secret exit at the rear. Carron told me about that, but he made no mention of the exact spot where it comes out, and it would be too risky trying to get in that way, there are too many tunnels in that hillside, we would lose our way for a certainty.'

'Any chance of sneaking up on them without being seen, through those trees you mentioned on top of the rise?' asked Barton, the sheriff of Carson.

'Not unless we manage to do it under cover of darkness and even then it might not pay off. They have a look out permanently on top of that rise and he can see in both directions for several miles. But it's the only way we can do it. We've got to attack at night, when there's no moon. I'd prefer it if we could make a diversionary move to draw some of them away. It'll make it easier for us to overcome those left behind. We can take care of the others when they return.'

'I reckon that could be arranged.' Bateson looked across at Barton, who nodded slowly. 'I don't know how these outlaws get their information. Obviously there's someone, either in Carson or here, who's giving them details of everything the stage is carrying. If we could only discover his identity, it would give us another lead.'

'What makes you so sure that it's a man,' asked Dan quietly. 'It could quite easily be a woman, you know.'

'I hadn't thought of that. D'you suspect anyone, Dan?'

'At the moment – no. It could be anyone.'

'Then we don't have much to go on, do we?' said Barton. 'There are close on a couple of thousand people in Carson. It could be any one of them.'

'There are quite a lot that we can eliminate at once,' retorted Dan hotly. 'Only those who had any access to that strongbox or the records of the Wells Fargo office, could know what is in it every day. That narrows things down quite a lot.' He turned to Bateson. 'Do you figure you could spare a couple of men to look into that, Sheriff? It oughtn't to be—'

'Now just a minute, young man,' interrupted Barton heatedly. 'You're taking a lot on to yourself, aren't you? Carson is my territory. If anyone gives the orders there, I'll be doing it. Just who do you figure you are, anyway, coming here and telling us what to do.'

For a moment, Dan felt tempted to reveal his true identity to the other, then suppressed the urge. There was a lot more he needed to know and for that, it was essential that he should continue to work under cover with only Bateson aware of who he really was. For the time being, it was sufficient if the other thought him to be nothing more than a busybody, trying to push his way into things.

'I'm not a lawman, if that's what you mean,' he said smoothly. 'But I do have certain interests in these parts, and they include seeing that anything I send on the Wells Fargo stages gets through, without being taken by this outlaw gang operating in the territory. I managed to get myself captured by the Sheriff here and the gang fell for it. I now know where their hide-out is. Seeing that I'm the only man here who does, I think that entitles me to special consideration.'

'Mebbe it does, young fella. But don't you get any high ideas. Don't forget that I'm sheriff of Carson. I'll arrange for this to be looked into, though I can't promise anything. There are quite a lot of people who have access to those files and whoever it is, he's been clever enough to escape detection so far.'

'All right, but in the meantime, we have to work out a

plan to get most of them away from that cave. If we can reach there after nightfall and take the guards they leave behind, the rest will be easy.'

Bateson spoke up harshly: 'I guess we can spread it around that we'll be running a night shipment through from Carson. Word will get through to them and they'll be waiting somewhere along the trail for a stage that never shows up. While they're waiting, we'll move through the desert and get there about nightfall.'

'That could be the answer,' agreed Barton slowly. He still looked doubtful, but made no objections, 'Do you need any of my men with you, Bateson?'

'I reckon we can raise a posse in Shannon City. There are a lot a ranchers around these parts who've suffered losses because of this gang. They'll willingly spare some men to help us hunt them down.'

'When are you figuring on making your play?' asked Barton. 'You'll have to strike soon, catch them off balance.'

'First you'll have to spread that rumour around about the night shipment,' said Dan. 'Once you've done that and there seems a real chance that they've fallen for it, get a telegraph message through to us. We'll be waiting to act the minute we get the word.'

The other made for the door, opened it and stepped out on to the boardwalk. He gave a quick nod. 'Keep on the alert,' he said, and his voice was low and seriously deep. 'I know these men. They're born killers, vicious and ruthless. If anything should go wrong, you'll never get a second chance. They know you now, Trafford. You'll be a marked man from this minute on.'

'Sure, I know, Sheriff. I'll be watching OK.' Dan watched as the other climbed into the saddle of one of the waiting horses and galloped off along the dusty main street. A lot dependeds on the sheriff of Carson, he thought reflectively; but this was the only chance they had now. Perhaps he, himself, was the only one who knew just what they were up against, what they would have to overcome, once they reached that hide-out in the rocks, out in the middle of the desert to the south. Going back inside, he looked across at Bateson. The other men began to file out of the office, moving across to the saloon around the corner to slake their thirst.

'Reckon we ought to question Jeb Carron,' said Bateson after a brief pause. 'Could be that we can get something outa him.'

Dan shrugged and followed the other along the short passage leading to the cells at the rear of the building. He doubted if Jeb would talk now that he knew how he had been tricked. When they reached the cell, Jeb Carron was seated on the edge of the low bunk, his head in his hands. He looked up swiftly, with an expression of animal cunning on his swarthy features as he heard their footsteps and his lips drew back into a thin snarl when he saw Dan. 'You'll pay for this. you g'damned lawman,' he snarled viciously. 'Don't think you'll get away with it. Luke'll be on your trail from now on. There ain't no place big enough for yuh to hide in the whole territory. And when he does catch up with yuh, he'll see that you suffer before you die.'

'He's got to catch me first,' said Dan coolly. 'And I'm betting that when we do meet face to face again, the boot will be on the other foot. You're forgetting that l know the location of our hide-out, and somehow I doubt whether Luke will move from there. He'll be relying on spotting us a long ways off and being ready for us.'

'Yeah.' The other got to his feet and came towards the cell door, huge hands reaching out and gripping the metal bars tightly as if determined to shake them loose from their foundations. 'And he'll cut you down like prairie dogs long before you get there.' He turned to Sheriff Bateson. 'Go ahead,' he sneered. 'Get your posse together and ride out. See how many of you manage to get back once Luke's made his play with you.'

Bateson shook his head slowly, 'We ain't fools, Carron. We know what we're doing and this time, it'll be Luke who gets the surprise.'

A little of the sneering contempt faded from the other's face and there was a fresh expression, which Dan could not read, in the narrow, close-set eyes.

'You're bluffing,' he said finally. 'You're just saying that so's I'll talk. Well you'll get nothin' outa me. Let's see how far you get with this fella leading your posse. Sure he knows the way, but once he gets there, he's finished. Luke'll be expecting you any time.'

'You'd better talk,' said Dan softly. 'Luke won't be there when we make the attack. And we'll be moving in under cover of darkness. I reckon we ought to be able to get close enough without being seen.'

'Luke won't fall for anything like that and you know it,' snarled the other. He went back and lowered himself on to the bunk eyeing them from beneath lowered brows. 'There ain't anything you could do to trick him out into the open.'

'Not even if we spread it around in Carson that the stage would be taking his brother there for trial?'

From the other's sudden silence, Dan knew that he had hit the one spot where Luke Carron was vulnerable.

The telegraph message came two days later from Sheriff Barton. Dan acted quickly. Within the hour, a posse had been formed from men spared by the ranchers in the surrounding territory and late that afternoon, they rode out of Shannon City, heading south into the inhospitable desert which stretched almost clear to the state border. There were twenty men in the posse, all handy with their guns, all determined to end, once and for all, the menace of the Carron gang. With Jeb Carron safely locked way in the jailhouse, they needed only to take his brother, dead or alive, and Dan felt that the rest of the gang would disintegrate. Leaderless, with their hide-out discovered, he was certain that they would leave the area, those who were still alive after the coming night.

Out in the desert, they kept the lowering sun on their right hand, riding swiftly, but not hurriedly, their horses' hooves sounding dully in the sand and rough scrubland. Dan rode with eyes slitted against the flooding glare of the sun, keeping a sharp look out for any of the gang. If Luke had fallen for the news they had deliberately spread around Carson, it was possible that he might be in the vicinity, and here in the desert, it was easy to see for several miles in any direction. But as the minutes dragged on into hours, and they saw no one at all, he began to lose some of the feeling of apprehension which had been dragging at the corner of his mind ever since they had ridden out of Shannon City.

Four miles south of the town, they passed through an area of broken, wooden huts, perched at the bottom of a broad ridge. Here, there had once been a small, thriving community, where a score or so miners had panned the narrow streams for gold and worked the long abandoned mines for the precious metal. But all that had been the best part of twenty years ago, and now there were only the roofless huts to give a mute witness to what had once happened there. What had once been the mine was now only a dark tunnel leading into the rock which lifted to a height of perhaps fifty feet or so above the flatness of the surrounding desert. There was a pile of wooden poles in the opening beyond which the discoloured railings dump slanted off towards the desert itself.

Bateson squinted up at the sun, gave a quick nod. 'We ought to be getting within sight of those mine workings in an hour, Dan,' he said reflectively. 'Think we ought to rest up a while. The horses are tired and we don't want to get within sight of the place until after dark.'

'Reckon you're right, Sheriff. There ought to be a small waterhole in that direction, about a quarter of a mile further on. We could camp there for an hour or so. Not much more daylight left, I guess.'

For the next hour, they rested beside the muddy water-hole, checking their weapons and their position on the old surveyor's map which Bateson had brought along. All of the men in the posse knew what to do and Dan felt certain that they would do it without the necessity for further orders. The ground evidence so far indicated that no one had used this trail for several weeks. Obviously the Carron gang were not in the habit of using it. When they finally rode away from the waterhole, it was almost dark. The sun had set below the western horizon a quarter of an hour before, leaving only a swiftly-dying red stain to mark the place where it had gone down. From the east, the darkness was spreading in swiftly, covering the sky and bringing with it a cool wind which swept down from the north.

'We leave the horses tethered out in the desert once we get within half a mile of that ridge,' said Dan quietly. 'And then go the rest of the way on foot. And whatever happens, I want no noise, That guard will still be there even after dark and he has only to hear the faintest sound to give the alarm.'

'The men nodded. They had been chosen carefully for their knowledge of tracking, their ability to move through dense undergrowth without snapping a single twig, without giving away their presence until it was too late. But it needed only one man to put a foot wrong for their plan to be useless,

The low range of hills on the horizon was little more than a darker smudge as they rode up, the sand muffling any sound of their approach. They left their horses tethered to a stake in the ground and went forward in a half crouch. As he moved swiftly in front of the others, leading the way, Dan wondered what they might find as they climbed that ridge and went in through the trees. Had Luke Carron fallen for their trick? Or was he still there, with the rest of his outlaws, waiting for them to make their play? Everything seemed to depend upon so many things and there was a riot of half-formed thoughts and ideas teeming through his brain as they reached the base of the low hills and crouched there for several moments, listening intently. Straining his ears, Dan tried to pick out any sound from the trees above them, but everything was quiet and still, except for the faint breeze which blew through

61

the branches and stirred the leaves.

Finally, he was satisfied and waved his arm to motion the others to follow close behind him, They entered the thick cover of the undergrowth and moved up towards the top of the ridge. They had come upon it a little to the north of the spot where Dan and the outlaws had ridden in several days before, but he had seen enough then to know his way around, even in the dark. He also knew where they would come upon the outlaw acting as look-out and as they neared the top of the ridge, he motioned the men to remain where they were while he slithered forward alone, moving with the quiet stealth of an Indian. A dark shadow, he slipped between the trees, his hand closing on his gun, easing it out of its holster. Reversing it, he clutched it by the long barrel and was behind the solitary guard before the other knew that anything was wrong. Swiftly, he brought the butt of the gun down with a soggy thud on the top of the man's head, caught him as he fell and lowered his body carefully into the brush. Less than five seconds had passed and there had not been a single sound loud enough to warn the rest of the outlaws who might be inside the cave.

Going back, he gestured to the posse to work their way forward and a few moments later, they had worked their way over the ridge and were on the narrow, winding trail which led downwards, towards the desert which lay beyond and then along the side of the hills, turning sharply into the hidden entrance of the cave.

This was going to be the tricky part. If they succeeded in getting inside the entrance of the cave before being seen, they stood a good chance of shooting it out with the outlaws on more than even terms; but if they were all caught out in the open, then things could turn bad for them. They reached the bottom of the slope and Dan stood a little on one side to motion in the direction of the cave. Three of the men had slipped past him when it happened. With a suddenness that was startling, in spite of the fact that Dan had been half-expecting it, the silence of the night erupted with gunfire. The brief stabbing flashes of light from the barrels of the guns were in the direction of the cave and the rocks which lay piled around it.

With a savage, bitter oath, he flung himself to the ground as lead fanned his cheek. They had been discovered and now everything depended on getting inside that cave as soon as possible.

'Spread out and take them from both sides,' he said harshly, speaking loudly so that everyone could hear. 'And keep under cover.' There was no point in maintaining silence now that the outlaws knew exactly where they were. Quickly, he ran forward, head low, shoulders hunched as he ran from tree to tree, feet slipping in his haste to get within killing distance of the enemy. By now, his eyes were accustomed to the pitch blackness of the moonless night and he could just make out the two dark shapes which moved less than twenty yards away, among the boulders in front of the old mine workings. His guns jumped into his hands as he thumbed the triggers, firing swiftly and instinctively at the fleeting, gliding shapes. He heard one of the outlaws cry out and saw him fall forward, but it was impossible from that distance to tell whether the wound had been fatal or not.

There was a deep and burning anger inside him as he eased himself forward with slow, deliberate movements. Those men had been waiting for them to show themselves and that meant only one thing; they had known all about this attack from the very beginning. It had been pure luck and good frontiersmanship that had enabled him to kill that guard on top of the hill. There was a little germ of suspicion beginning to crystallize at the back of his mind but for the moment it refused to come out into the open so that he might recognize it for what it was. Then he had thrust it into the back of his mind and was concentrating every sense on trying to pick out the whereabouts of the men who had fired on them; and how many there were inside the cave. Even if Luke Carron had known beforehand of this attack, he might still have pulled out after that stage, knowing that two or three men, well placed inside the mine workings, could hold off the sheriff and his posse through the night and the next day if necessary.

Sheriff Bateson came crawling up beside him in the darkness and whispered hoarsely. 'Reckon there can't be more than three men in there at the most, Dan. Think we can go in after them?'

He shook his head quickly. 'That would be asking for trouble, Sheriff. Once in there they can pick off any man who tries to rush 'em, Make no mistake about that. We'll have to play this hand real careful.'

'You got a plan in your mind, Dan?'

'Could be. There's a narrow trail leading over the top of the entrance. I spotted it one morning while I was there. It doesn't lead anywhere. My guess is they used it to carry the piles over for shoring up the roof of the tunnels. If we could get up there without being seen and then lure them out into the open—'

'It's worth a try anyway, Dan,' agreed the other. 'Lead the way and I'll follow you. Better warn the others what we're going to do first. Don't figure on being shot at by one of the posse in mistake for an outlaw.'

Loose rock on the narrow, torturous trail made movement difficult as Dan led the way over the top of the cave entrance. Treacherous and slippery, he had to pause several times to maintain his balance and he knew that it would he ten times worse for the older man who crawled so doggedly on his heels, determined not to let him down. In the darkness, he skinned the backs of his hands and knees on jutting outcrops of sharp-edged rock which tore into his flesh. Bateson's harsh breathing was so loud that it seemed impossible for any of the outlaws down below not to hear it. The rest of the men, spread out among the rocks and the trees, were firing continuously now, deliberately keeping their fire low to avoid any possibility of hitting the two men crawling along the treacherous ledge.

At any moment, Dan expected a loose rock to slide

from beneath his hands or feet and go bouncing down into the cave entrance below, warning the men down there of what was taking place above their heads. It was as soon as he reached a point almost immediately over the entrance that Dan noticed the dark shadows directly below him. His quick glance told him that there were four of them, lying down there among the rocks, their bodies almost inside the cave. One of them was lying very still, taking no part in the shooting and he guessed that this was the man he had shot. The three others were still very much alive and were forcing the men among the trees to keep their heads down.

It wouldn't be long before the posse used up all of their ammunition and when that happened, they would be forced to withdraw. As for the bandits, he had no doubts about the fact that they had plenty of ammunition stached away inside the cave. He had seen that much for himself. Evidently, Luke Carron had planned things well in advance when he had set up this hide-out.

Giving quick scrutiny to the positions of the men below him, Dan figured that with luck, and cover from the sheriff, he ought to be able to take two of the men down there among the rocks. If there were any others still inside the old workings, it might make things awkward, but that was a chance he would have to take. Leaning sideways, he whispered his intentions to Bateson, saw the other's quick nod indicating that he understood, then lifted himself quickly to his feet, pausing for a moment poised on the very lip of the cave entrance. The man immediately below him never stood a chance. Dan landed right on top of him, heard the other's sharp grunt of pain as the heels of his boots struck in the small of his back. Before either of the other outlaws had time to turn their heads, he had clubbed the man in the back of the head and was rolling sideways before the shots from their guns flicked out with stabbing red flames in the darkness.

Bateson had held his fire for a moment for fear of hitting him, but seeing him roll away out of harm, he began firing instantly. One of the outlaws suddenly yelled savagely and stumbled to his feet, clutching at his arm.

Another of the Sheriff's bullets took him in the fleshy part of the right leg and he went down hard as it gave way under his weight.

Dan heard bullets whistle around him as he dived for cover, the thin screaming of the ricochets whining in his ears. There was no doubt now that there was at least one man back there in the cave, and, regardless of the fact that he might hit one of his own men by mistake in the darkness, he was shooting blind, hoping to hit Dan. More gunfire deafened the air as Dan crouched down among the rocks. For the moment, he was safe from the bullets of the outlaws, but they had now switched their fire to where Bateson lay above the cave. There was very little cover up there and if the sheriff was not to be killed, it was essential that Dan should do something to distract their attention back to himself. Not trying to get up, realizing that with the man back there in the cave he would never make it, he fired from where he lay, thumbing the triggers back as fast as they would go. Out of the corner of his eye, he saw the nearer of the men suddenly rear up from the shadow of the rocks, arms flailing high over his head as if trying to clutch at an invisible something just above his head. His guns fell from nerveless fingers, clattering on to the rocks as he toppled forward with a bullet in his chest. His companion, crouched down out of sight a little distance away, snapped a couple of shots in Dan's direction, but these merely sang viciously off the smooth surface of the rocks and went whining away into the darkness.

Already, the rest of the men of the posse were closing in, sensing that the kill was imminent. They came firing, but picking their targets carefully, knowing that he was there somewhere. Dan knew that he could safely leave the man, still alive, to their guns and, turning swiftly on his heel, still not lifting his head, he slithered towards the inside of the cave. There was still one of the outlaws in there, possibly two. Whether or not Luke Carron was around, keeping in the background until he was sure of which way the fight was going, he did not know. But he wanted to get that man back there before he had a chance to flee along that dark tunnel, through the hill and out into the desert a couple of miles away, where there would probably be a horse waiting, a horse which could take him out, not only to freedom, but possibly to where Luke Carron was, to give him the news.

Inside the cave, there was silence now. Nothing seemed to move in the almost pitch blackness. There had been a fire but the embers had been crushed out by a heavy boot at the first sound of shooting. He knew that the man who had shot at him from inside was not dead, not even wounded. If he was still there, determined to shoot it out with him, then the outlaw had the distinct advantage of being able to see him against the lighter background of the sky. In addition, he would know his way around, know every rock and boulder.

Very cautiously, Dan felt his way forward, one six-gun in its holster, the other balanced in his right hand. His finger was hard on the trigger, every nerve in his body screaming with the rising tension, every muscle tight with anticipation. Strangely, there was none of the exhilaration he often felt, stalking a killer like this. Instead, his mind felt dull and in the forefront of it, there was the growing conviction that he had forgotten something very important, that events were happening somewhere else that he ought to know of.

There was a faint sound to his right and he paused instantly, body freezing into immobility. It had been scarcely a sound at all, merely the faintest scrape of metal on the rock, as if the front sight of a revolver had touched the rock for a fraction of a second. But to his trained ears, it had been enough to pinpoint the position of the outlaw. Very slowly, Dan turned his head, trying to make out details in the gloom. From outside the cave, there came a volley of shots, then silence. Evidently the outlaw had been pinned down and then killed. Crouching down, he could just make out the jumbled pile of boulders which stood in the far corner of the cave and almost directly in front of him, the shape of the large table which had been turned on to its side. His lips curled into a tight grin. That was the most obvious place for a man to hide if he intended to shoot down anyone entering the cave He waited for the other to lift his head, the revolver poised in his hand. He was debating whether to make the first move, to force the other into the open, when there was the sharp clatter of someone coming into the cave almost directly behind him.

'You in there, Dan?' Bateson's harsh voice. The words echoed around the cave, and the next instant, they were drowned by the thunderous explosion of a gunshot. Dan flattened himself against the cold rock, biting off the curse which had risen unbidden to his lips when the other had called out, exposing himself to the outlaw's gun. For that gunshot had come, not from behind the table where he had expected the outlaw to be, but from among the rocks, over to his right. The brief orange stab of flame had caught his attention immediately and he knew, with a sick certainty that if it had not been for Bateson yelling like that, if he had gone ahead with his plan to force the outlaw into the open, he would have been shot down before he had taken a step towards that table. It had been a trick on the part of the outlaw and it had almost worked.

Now that he knew where the man lay hiding, he slithered forward cautiously. Working his way upwards among the boulders, moving more by touch than sight, he came upon a point just behind where he judged the other to be, less than three feet from where the muzzle flash had come.

There was a faint sound in the cave entrance as more of the men came up, clearly not sure what to do. He thought he heard Bateson's voice telling them not to fire, that he was inside. Silence clung like a sable shroud around everything, so that he could almost hear his own heart thumping against his ribs. The strain was beginning to tell, but it was the outlaw who broke first. There was the sudden scrape of a boot against the rock and a second later, he saw the man's head lift from among the boulders. Gently, he snaked forward, then cocked the hammer of his gun with a sharp, ominous click.

'Don't make any sudden moves, *hombre*,' he said quietly. 'I've got a gun on your back and my trigger finger is getting itchy.'

He heard the other's sharp intake of breath, saw the man stiffen involuntarily, then went on: 'Drop your guns and then stand forward where I can see you.'

There was a moment's pause, then the clatter of guns striking the rocks. The man moved forward, hands clasped on top of his Stetson. Dan got to his feet, came up behind him and pushed him forward.

'OK Sheriff. He's all yours,' he called, the barrel of his gun hard against the other's back.

'Looks like we cleaned up most of them, Dan,' said Bateson, as he came into the cave. 'Sure this is the only one?'

'Unless the others got away through the tunnel at the back of the cave.'

'If they did, we don't stand much chance of catching them now. By dawn, I guess they'll be miles away from here, probably heading for the Texas border as fast as their mounts will take them.'

'Any sign of Luke Carron?'

'Nope. Seems like he wasn't here. He must have headed out like we figured. But why go alone?'

'He could have reasoned that he might be able to scout things out better by himself. It's pretty obvious that he was tipped off about this night attack. Those men were ready and waiting for us. He probably figured that the five of them would be enough to hold us and for his business, he needed nobody.'

'Guess he's got another think coming.' There was a note of tired exultation in Bateson's tone. 'This ought to smash the Carron gang for good. With Jeb in the jailhouse and all of them finished except for Luke, it's my guess that he'll hit the trail out of the territory.'

Dan pressed his lips tightly together, 'I'd like to believe that,' he said slowly, 'but somehow that doesn't sound like Luke. He's got something up his sleeve though I'm damned if I can figure out what it is.'

'When he does catch up with you, Clayton, or whatever your name really is,' snarled the man they had captured, 'he'll make you wish you'd never been born. He knows how you double-crossed him and how you caught his brother, Jeb. He won't rest until he's paid you back for that.'

'Don't reckon he can do much on his own,' said Dan easily. He peered into the man's face and recognised him as Clem, the man who had been with Jeb and himself on the trail when they had tried to hold up the stage. 'Just where is Luke at the moment?'

'Wouldn't you like to know that?' sneered the other savagely. 'If you think I'm going to tell you anything, you're wrong, mister. All I want to see, is you at the end of a rope, which is where you'll be if Luke gets you.'

'I reckon you'd better talk,' said Bateson fiercely. 'If'n you don't, you'll hang with Jeb. There's a whole string of charges against you, ranging from armed robbery to murder. You won't be able to talk your way outa those.'

'You don't scare me, Sheriff. I've been broken outa better jails than yours by Luke. He can do it again.'

'Not this time,' assured Dan. 'This time you'll face trial and then I'll personally see to it that the sentence is carried out. The west has no place for killers like you any longer. We're going to clean it up – and good. Pretty soon, whether you and your kind like it or not, this country is going to be a safe and decent place for people to live.'

They took the outlaw out of the cave, located the gang's horses tethered to a rope strung between two of the trees a little distance from the cave.

'Get into the saddle,' said Dan quietly, 'and don't try to make a break for it. Some of these men have lost a lot because of your activities and they're just waiting for some excuse to shoot you down,'

The look on the other's face told Dan more than words that the man knew that what he had said was the truth. As they rode out through the desert, with the stars twinkling brilliantly in the cloudless sky which stretched in a wide, clear arch over their heads, Dan had the feeling that, for the first time since he had arrived in this territory, things were going to be different, far better than they had been before. He had managed to bring most of the men of the Carron gang to justice. True some of them lay back there at the old mine workings, buzzard-meat, but that was no more than they had deserved. The old order here was beginning to change. The outlaws and brigands who had tried to dominate the west, the frontier towns which were still in their infancy, had had their little day. Now, law and order were coming to the far West. 'The homesteaders were moving in, the big prairie ranches were being gradually broken up. Towns and cities would be built here someday once they got the railroad through and the roads were improved so that the stages could roll in on time.

But there was still something troubling him, something he couldn't quite put his finger on. Where was Luke Carron? He was the most dangerous man in that whole outfit, far more dangerous than that killer they had left behind bars in the jailhouse. He was still out there on the loose somewhere, possibly knowing that his men had been killed or taken prisoner and even now, he might be planning his revenge on the man who had tricked him, had led the sheriff and his posse across the desert and inflicted this defeat on him.

Luke Carron had fought in the war, had been an officer with the South, and a setback like this he would regard as only temporary. There were still plenty of men in this wild territory willing to follow a man like him, someone who could offer them the chance to kill and plunder. Whatever happened, Luke Carron had to be found, taken in dead or alive.

During the fighting, only one man in the posse had been hit. A bullet had taken him in the shoulder and although the wound had bled a lot, the bullet had come out through the back and it looked more dangerous than it really was. It was almost dawn when they sighted Shannon City. The long ride across the emptiness of the desert had forced their horses to a flagging shuffle and the men themselves were heavy-eyed with lack of sleep. As they rode into the main street, Dan looked about him keenly. There was that feeling back in his mind, the impression that there was something wrong. But it was not until they turned the corner and rode towards the jailhouse, that he knew what it was, knew what had been nagging at the edges of his brain all that night.

Three men lay on the boardwalk with several of the citizens standing over them. They looked up as Dan and the sheriff rode towards them, with the rest of the posse moving up behind.

'Looks like trouble,' said Dan tightly. He urged his mount forward, slid to the street in front of the sheriff's office. Going forward, he caught hold of one of the men by the shoulder and asked tightly: 'What happened here?'

'They came in about an hour ago. There was scarcely anyone around and we couldn't stop them.'

'Go on,' rasped Dan harshly. He realized that his fingers were biting into the man's flesh through the cloth of his coat and relaxed his grip a little. 'How many were there? Did they get through into the jailhouse?'

'There were only two of them. Masked men who rode into town from the north. They shot down those three men in cold blood, then went inside the office. When they came out they had another man with them, one of the prisoners, I guess.'

'Luke Carron.' The words were jerked from Bateson's lips. He went inside the office while Dan examined the three men lying on the boardwalk. One glance was enough to tell him that all three were dead. They had been shot down at close range. None of them had stood

72

any chance at all. Tightening his lips into a thin, hard line, he straightened up as Bateson came hurrying out of the office,

One glance at the sheriff's face told him what he had feared.

'Jeb Carron,' he said thinly. 'He's gone. He's been busted outa jail by that brother of his.'

Behind them, Clem laughed harshly. 'I told you, Sheriff. Luke's a lot smarter than any of yuh. Seems like while you were back at the cave, he was in here busting his brother outa jail. He'll come gunning for you very soon.'

Dan said nothing. Inwardly, he was too busy trying to figure out who that other man had been, the man who had ridden into Shannon City with Luke Carron.

CHAPTER FOUR

THUNDER IN THE GUNSMOKE

'WE ought to have figured that Luke Carron would try something like this,' said Bateson and there was a note almost of self-accusation in his tone. 'What I'd like to know is how he knew we were headed that way. If we hadn't been g'darned lucky, we could have been pinned down there all night, by those five men. I reckon that was what he was counting on. Getting his brother outa jail and then riding back to the mine, hoping to take us by surprise from the rear. Even with the men we had, that could have turned the trick. We'd have had little enough ammunition left by that time.' He eased himself into a more comfortable position in the chair, resting his elbows on the top of the table. Outside, beyond the window, the town was coming to life. The bodies of the three men, killed by the outlaws had been taken away, but there were still a few curious bystanders that Dan could see through the window, watching the place where violent death had come just recently.

Dan's brow was knit in worried thought. Little ideas kept turning themselves over and over in his mind. That the man who had ridden into Shannon City with Carron had been their informant from Carson, he did not doubt.

There had been no other person able to help him break his brother from the jail. If only they knew the identity of this man who kept himself so much in the background, he had the idea that things would be a lot easier.

'You reckon those three could be headed back towards the old mine workings, Dan?' asked the other suddenly. His bushy black brows were drawn into a straight line. He fingered the bunch of keys absently.

'Could be. They might figure it to be the last place we'd go looking for them. Somehow, I doubt whether they'll be riding out of the territory. Carron has an outstanding score to settle.' He nodded at the other's interrogative lift of the dark brows. 'He means to kill me for what I did that day they planned to rob the stage. He'll never forget that I've been personally responsible for killing or taking prisoner almost the whole of the Carron gang.'

'So you figure that sooner or later, he'll come looking for you and all we have to do is keep an eye on you?' There was a tight grin on the other's face. 'You're taking one hell of a risk, Dan. There's got to be another way.'

'There isn't and you know it. One thing I might be able to do though. Go into Carson and see if I can get a lead on the man who's been giving Carron all of that information. I've a hunch who it might be, but I'll need proof before I can make a move.'

'You need any help at all, Dan, I'll get in touch with Barton and ask him to help you, officially. No need to tell him who you are, but a word from me might help.'

Dan shook his head. 'I reckon I can work better alone on this problem.' he said quietly. 'But first, I think I'll rest up for a couple of hours. If Carron acts the way I think he will, he'll bide his time until he's sure of success. He won't want to risk tangling with the law until he has a chance of winning.'

'Suit yourself, Dan. But be careful. There are still a few wild hellions in town who'd throw in their lot with Carron if they figured he could come out on top. For the moment, we've shown them that he can be beaten, but if he should get the whip hand again, he'll have more men behind him than he had before.'

'I'll be careful, Sheriff.' He made his way over to the saloon, pushed open the doors, threw a swift glance around the bar, then went over. Kitty Masters appeared at the top of the stairs just as he reached the bar and swept down them, the long train of her dress spread out behind her. In spite of her mountainous, fleshy figure, he had to admit that there was something regal about the way she walked and held herself. She came up to the bar beside him and laid a jewelled hand on his arm, turning towards the bartender.

'Mister Trafford's drinks are on the house, Charlie,' she said imperiously. 'He can have anything he likes, and pour me one too.'

While Dan sipped his drink, she regarded him whimsically out of the corner of her eye. 'Seems we had you figured all wrong,' she said quietly, her husky voice low. 'You surprised everybody when you lit out with that outlaw gang and then showed up by saving the stage. They tell me too that you managed to break up the Carron gang out there in the desert, but that the two brothers are still very much alive. Aren't you afraid they'll come after you for revenge?'

He gave her a straight stare and although she was accustomed to handling men, it was Kitty's eyes that first looked away from that disconcerting gaze. 'I'm hoping they will come after me,' he said firmly. 'And when they do, I'll be ready for them, If they stay around in the territory, it may be the only way we have of catching them.'

'You're offering yourself as gun-bait in the hope of capturing them?' There was only a trace of surprise in her voice. 'And I thought you had a little horse-sense. Don't you know what kind of killers they are? Those brothers don't fight fair. They don't give a man an even shake. They'd as soon shoot you in the back from ambush as gun you down in the street and either way they won't give you the chance to draw.'

'Whatever happens, I don't reckon they'll make their play for a day or so. In that time, there's a lot I have to do over in Carson.' He drained his glass, set it down on the bar and watched as the bartender filled it up again at a quick nod from Kitty. He turned to face her.

'They told me back in Carson that you were one of the biggest property owners in the territory, but that you went in for the mines around here. Is that true Kitty?'

'Sure, it's true. A woman has to look out for herself when she gets to my age.' She laughed throatily at his glance. 'There's no need to be embarrassed because I'm long since past the age of being a young girl, Mister Trafford. I know what I am and I know what the rest of the townsfolk think I am. They hate my guts.'

He shrugged. 'It's immaterial to me how much you own,' he said calmly. 'But I was wondering if you could help me. You're over in Carson quite often. You must know a lot of the townspeople there too, almost as well as you do those in Shannon City.'

'I reckon that's true.' She eyed him over the rim of her glass. 'What is it you want to know?'

'How well do you know Sheriff Barton?'

If she was surprised at the question she certainly gave no outward sign. Her face did not change as she glanced down at her glass, the light from the overhead chandelier glistening off the rings on her fingers. 'Sheriff Barton,' she said quietly, glancing round to make sure that the bartender had moved away and was no longer within earshot. 'He's a strange man. Not the usual type of lawman we've had in these parts. He came to Carson about three years ago, just after they built the Wells Fargo office and started a regular stage run through to Shannon City and beyond.'

'You think he's a regular lawman?'

This time there was definite surprise on her rouge-and-painted face. Her eyes widened a little. 'You've got an idea that he isn't?' she asked incredulously.

He shrugged his shoulders a little. 'Let's say that it's

nothing more than a hunch at the moment,' he went on. 'But there are one or two things that point to him being implicated with the Carrons.'

'What sort of things?' She filled her glass herself from the bottle on the bar, at the same time motioning the bartender to remain where he was with a quick wave of her hand. Her eyes had narrowed slightly and Dan wondered what thoughts were running through her clever, scheming brain. He hoped that he had not done the wrong thing in taking her into his confidence.

'For instance, when Sheriff Bateson and I worked out the plan for catching the gang on the wrong foot, Barton was there in the office when we discussed it. He knew when and where we intended to strike. And those men at the hide-out had been warned.'

'It could have been any one of the other men you had in the office at that time,' she countered.

He shook his head. 'All of those men came from Shannon City,' he said harshly. 'I checked on that later. Barton was the only one from Carson, and it is someone there who's been giving Carron the information about the strongbox carried on the stage. Barton's in a position where he could get that kind of information quite easily. He could be one of Carron's men, planted in the sheriff's office some time ago.'

'It's possible,' admitted the other. 'But you won't find it easy to prove it. How are you going to set about it?'

'That's something I'm not clear on at the moment. I hope to sleep on it and see if I can't come up with some idea before tonight.'

'I kept your room ready, just in case you did show up again. There was some talk around town that you were dead, that those gunhawks had killed you and left your body out there to rot in the desert. Seems that was just wishful thinking on their part. You look tough enough and I heard you were pretty quick with your gun. Just where do you fit into all this? You could be a lawman, but I ain't seen no badge. On the other hand, this might be something personal. The Carrons used to live here just before the war. They carried out a lot of crooked deals and you might come from one of the families they ruined.'

He shook his head, smiling a little at the obvious way in which she was trying to drag information out of him. 'Nothing like that,' he said quietly, as he turned towards the stairs. 'But I'd be grateful if you'd keep what I've told you a secret. The fewer people who know I'm headed for Carson, the better.'

'You secret is safe with me, cowboy,' she said softly. 'But whatever you do, don't understimate Luke Carron. He's a shrewd and clever man. Just because you've broken up the gang, doesn't mean that you've finished him in these parts.'

'I'll remember that – and thanks for the warning.' He made his way up the wide stairs, conscious of her glance following him. Letting himself into his room, he threw a swiftly-embracing glance through the window, looking along the street in both directions, then undid his bandana, unbuckled the gunbelt and laid it on the chair close beside the bed. Outside, the sun was climbing steadily into the blue clearness of the sky and he twitched the heavy curtains across the window before pulling off his boots and stretching himself out on the bed. Although his body craved for sleep, it was a long time in coming. His mind was too full of other things to allow him to rest.

There was the urgent need for action. With those two killers still running around on the loose somewhere in the desert to the south of Shannon City, no one was safe until they had been caught or killed. After a long while, he fell asleep, waking late in the afternoon with the sun already sinking down out of sight behind the buildings on the opposite side of the street. Swinging his legs to the floor, he got up, washed and shaved, put on a clean shirt, felt surprised that he was hungry again.

Going downstairs, he found only a few men in the bar. Shortly before dark, the others would come in, broad-shouldered cowpunchers from the neighbouring ranches, men riding herd along the trail which passed far to the north of the town; one or two prospectors from the hills further to the west, gaunt-eyed men who sought gold and never seemed to give up, ever striving to hit it rich, even though most of the veins had been worked clean many years before. But there was always a little of the precious metal to be found, a tiny trickle which kept them alive, filling their bellies with the cheap, rotgut whisky which was reserved specially for these men.

In one corner of the room, a poker game had begun, six men seated around the table. Dan recognized the man seated in one of the chairs, dealing the cards, as a professional gambler and wondered what kind of a shake the men playing with him would get. Like most men of his calibre, the gambler would be toting a short-barrelled gun in his dandy waistcost pocket and there would be a couple of his men among those at the bar, ready to cut loose with lead if a fight started over the deal.

A door at the far side of the room opened and Kitty Masters came in. She saw him immediately and came over, a smile creasing her fleshy features. 'Had a friend of yours in a little while ago asking about you,' she said.

He looked surprised. 'A friend?'

'That's right. Name of Stacey. Mean anything to you?'

He shook his head, his eyes perplexed, then remembered. 'Mary Stacey?'

'The same. She seemed worried.' The shrewd eyes watched him closely. 'You wouldn't be in love with the girl would you, Dan?'

'Good God, what makes you say that? I've only met her once, when the Carron gang attacked the stage. I've no idea why she should be worried about me. Did she say why she wanted to see me?'

'Nope. Just asked if you'd meet her at the store when you woke. Seemed to be something important.'

All thought of food was forgotten as he started for the door. Vaguely, he recalled that Mary Stacey's father was one of the biggest ranchers in the territory and wondered if that had anything to do with it. A man like that was bound to have plenty of enemies and it was more than likely that one of them was Luke Carron. He turned the corner of the street. The business of Sheriff Barton in Carson vanished temporarily from his mind. As usual, even here in Shannon City, he kept one part of his mind curiously detached from the rest, on his surroundings, and it was this that saved his life.

The man was crouched low on the timber roof of the livery stables on the far side of the street fifty yards or so ahead of him as he reached the boardwalk and moved forward. It was just a swift, fleeting glance, but enough for him to see the rifle in the man's hand and to realize that it was pointed in his direction, that this was a trap and unless he moved quickly and instinctively, he had only a few seconds in which to live. He twisted sideways, hitting the boardwalk with his left arm, felt the sharp stab of pain as he went down; then his right hand had clawed the gun from its holster and as he came up on to his knees, the rifle bullet smacked into the wooden wall just behind his head. Not trying to get to his feet, knowing that the man on the roof had plenty of time in which to fire again, he cut loose with lead from the ground. The range was extreme for a Colt, but he saw the man stagger a little, jerking as the slug hit him in the shoulder.

There was another crash of rifle fire, a burning sensation in his upper arm and then the man had clambered swiftly down the far side of the roof. Slowly, he pushed himself to his feet, gun still in his hand. There was no point in going after the would-be assassin, he reasoned. The man would have a horse waiting at the back of the livery stables and would be headed out of town long before he was able to get near enough even to try to identify him. Seconds later, he heard the sound of hoofbeats thundering into the distance and knew that he had surmised correctly.

A small crowd had gathered by this time, and a moment

later, Sheriff Bateson pushed his way through and came up to him. 'You all right, Dan?' His voice was anxious. 'I heard the shooting down at the office and came running. Did you see who it was who fired at you?'

Dan shook his head quickly, holstering the gun. 'He was on the roof of the livery stables. Used a rifle. I think I hit him in the shoulder, but it was only a flesh wound like this.' He grinned and ripped up the sleeve of his shirt. There was a smear of blood along his arm where the rifle bullet had ploughed through the flesh and glanced off the bone. It was not serious and would incapacitate him for only a few hours until the inevitable stiffness had worn off.

'Think it could have been one of the Carron brothers?' Bateson's tone was sharp. He looked at the faces of the people gathered on the boardwalk and in the street, but they all shook their heads. Even if one of them had recognised the would-be killer, Dan doubted if they would talk. The name of Carron still struck fear into them, even though the others were now on the run.

'Perhaps you'd better let Doc Travers take a look at that arm of yours,' suggested Bateson.

'Not just yet,' said Dan tightly. 'There's something I have to find out first. That could have been a trap someone laid for me just then. I want to make sure.'

'How do you figure on doing that?' queried the other, lowering his bushy black brows.

'Mary Stacey left word I was to meet her at the store as soon as I woke. I was on my way there when I ran into that ambush. I'd like to know if she had anything to do with it.'

'Mary!' There was stunned surprise in the Sheriff's voice. 'But that's impossible, Dan. I'll swear she had nothing to do with that attempt on your life. I've known her since she was knee-high to a grasshopper. She'd never do anything like that.'

'We'll see,' said Dan grimly. He walked quickly along the boardwalk with the Sheriff at his heels. Reaching the store he looked about him quickly, then saw the girl waiting inside, seated on one of the stools at the counter.

He went inside. She saw him at once and got quickly to her feet, a rosy flush spreading over her features. Standing there, with the sunlight streaming through the window, high-lighting her face, Dan had to admit that she was beautiful. Tall and willowy with a grace that was unusual in women who lived on the very frontier of civilization. He guessed that she had learned much of that back east.

'Mister Trafford. I'm so glad you came. I thought that—' She broke off as Sheriff Bateson pushed into the store, then looked back at Dan's grim face.

'Is something wrong?' Her hand went to her mouth as she saw the bloodstain on his shirt. 'That shooting. You've been hurt.'

'And I suppose that you knew nothing about it,' he said acidly. His gaze never left her face and he could have sworn that the surprise was genuine, but he could not afford to take chances now.

'What do you mean? I don't understand. Why should I know anything about it?'

'Whoever that man was who shot at me, he must have known I'd be coming along that way. Which means he knew I was going to meet you. Quite convenient, wasn't it? Lining me up as a target like that.'

For a moment she stared at him in unbelieving surprise, then a flush of anger touched her face and her eyes glinted dangerously. 'Mister Trafford,' she said thinly. 'I asked you to meet me because I thought you were the only man in the town who might be able to help me. It seems I made a big mistake. As for that man who shot at you back there, I know nothing about it, but it seems a great pity that he didn't put a bullet through that stupid head of yours.' She picked up her gloves from the counter, drew them on and started for the door.

She had only taken three paces when Dan caught her arm and said quietly: 'I'm sorry, Miss Stacey. I guess I shouldn't have said that. But when you've just been shot at, you aren't in the mood for thinking straight.'

She paused, seemed on the point of making another

sharp rejoinder, then relaxed. 'Very well, Mister Trafford.' Her lips curved into a faint smile. 'I suppose in the circumstances, it was quite a natural mistake.'

'That's better.' Dan grinned at her. 'Now, what was it you wanted to talk to me about? Something to do with the Carron gang?'

Her eyes widened a little, then she nodded. 'You're the first man we've had here who can stand against them,' she said slowly, going back to the counter and seating herself on the chair once more. 'As you probably know, my father owns one of the biggest ranches in the territory. He has more than ten thousand head of cattle, all prime beef, and makes regular shipments to the rail depot at Carson. I've been back east for three years so I've been out of touch with things lately. But I guessed from his letters that there was something wrong at the ranch, even though he tried to hide it from me. That's why I came back six months before he wanted me to. I had to find out for myself just what it was that was troubling him.'

'I see. And it was something to do with this outlaw gang?'

'That's right. I didn't realize until a few days ago how deeply he was involved with them. I thought at first that—'

'Your father involved with them, Miss Stacey?' He looked at her in surprise, then turned to the sheriff.

Bateson said: 'That doesn't sound like your father, Mary. I've known him all of my life. A hard man, but he's fair and honest. He'd never throw in his lot with polecats like the Carrons.'

The girl went on quickly: 'He isn't an outlaw, Sheriff. But they seem to have some kind of hold over him, so that he's forced to help them whether he wants to or not. I don't know what it is they have that can hurt him, but it must be something important or I'm sure he would turn them over to the Sheriff here whenever they ask him to hide them on the ranch. It's the last place anyone would think of looking for them.'

'Are they hiding out there now. Mary?' asked Bateson.

The girl shook her head. 'They were there last night,

but they rode out first thing this morning. I think they were headed south. I heard them talking together but I couldn't make out much of what they were saying and I didn't want them to know I was listening.'

'How many were there?' asked Dan. This explained why they had been unable to spot Luke and his brother riding south the previous night. Instead of making for the hide-out in the desert, they had ridden straight to the Stacey spread to the west of the town and holed up there for the night, forcing Bob Stacey to hide them, knowing that he would not turn them over to the law. His brow knit in thought as he tried to figure out what they might have had on Stacey to be able to force him to do this.

'There were just the two of them that I saw. I recognized one of them as Jeb Carron. The other man I'd never seen before.'

'That would have been his brother, Luke,' put in Bateson. 'Not much doubt about that. Sure you didn't see a third man around, Mary? Think carefully, this could be important.'

She paused, then shook her head. 'No, I'm sure there were only two. If there was a third he must have ridden off before reaching the house. He could have gone across the big meadow.'

'That's the way he would go if he were heading back towards Carson,' said Bateson tightly, 'Not much doubt about it, Dan.'

'You know who this third man was?' asked Mary Stacey.

'We've a hunch that he's Sheriff Barton from Carson, but we'll have to prove that before we can go any further,' said Dan tightly. 'Think you could warn the sheriff here if those men come back to the ranch?'

'I think so. It may not be easy. They watch all of us like hawks whenever they are there. I'll have to think up some excuse for coming into town,'

'Do your best, Mary,' said Dan quietly. He grinned down at her, 'And don't worry. We'll see this thing through and when we're finished, the Carron gang will be nothing

85

more than a bad dream for the folk in this neighbourhood. But don't mention our little talk to your father.
Those men may force him to talk and if he knows nothing,
he can tell them nothing.'

'I won't forget,' she promised. She looked hard at Dan
and the hardened lawman was the first to look away before
the calm gaze of those grey eyes. 'Take care of yourself,
Dan Trafford,' she went on softly as she walked towards
the door. 'We need men like you around these parts if
Shannon City is to grow and turn into a place for decent
citizens to live in.'

That night, Dan rode out of Shannon City and headed
east towards Carson. It was almost dark and the trail was
deserted as he put his mount to a gallop, intending to
cover the distance in as short a time as possible. He had
the feeling at the back of his mind that very soon, things
would come to a head as far as the Carron brothers were
concerned. Luke would be the one who wanted to bide his
time, choosing his opportunity carefully, but Jeb, smarting
under the insult of being taken prisoner and lodged in the
local jail, would advocate immediate action and for once,
Dan had the idea that Jeb might manage to overrule his
brother's more cautious nature.

By the time he rode into Carson, it was completely
dark, but there were a few lights in the place, although
the hour was late. He edged his mount warily along one
of the narrow side streets, keeping away from the main
street with its saloons and the sheriff's office which was his
first port of call. It was likely that he would find the sheriff in the saloon at that time of night. But first, there were
one or two records he wanted to check and he figured
that they would be locked away safely inside the sheriff's
desk.

The sound of a tinny tune being played on the piano
reached his ears from the direction of the saloon as he
worked his way towards the rear of the sheriff's office. Not
a single light showed in the building and he felt satisfied

that it was deserted. There might be one or two prisoners locked away in the cells but he did not figure on disturbing any of them.

Tethering his mount to a hitching post a little distance along the side street from the office, he dismounted and padded the rest of the way on foot, moving noiselessly with a catlike tread. After surveying the windows at the back of the office, he grinned to himself in the darkness. It was going to be easier breaking into this place than he had anticipated.

The thin blade of his knife made no sound as he inserted it between the edge of the window and the frame. Very gently, but exerting a steady pressure, he twisted it upward, heard the sharp explosive click as the lock snapped inside. A moment later, he had pushed up the window and climbed inside. Narrowing his eyes to accustom them to the gloom, he made out the low bed in the corner and the stand with the wash basin perched precariously upon it nearby. This must be the sheriff's bedroom, he guessed. Going over to the door, he opened it quietly, found himself in a long passage which he guessed ran past the cells. Fortunately, everything was in darkness and as he went forward, making no sound, there was no movement from any of the cells and he guessed that they were either empty or the occupants were asleep and caring little about who was prowling around the place.

In the office at the front of the building, the shuttered windows looking out on to the street would shut off any light and he lit the lamp on the desk in the corner of the room. There was no time for finesse. He burst the lock on the sheriff's drawer with the stout-bladed knife and riffled through the papers inside. Five minutes later, he was satisfied that the evidence he sought was not there. Impatiently, he glanced about him, looking for a likely hiding place for anything as important as that.

He searched the walls of the room thoroughly for any sign of a safe, but there was nothing. Biting his lip in indecision, he stood in the centre of the room, trying to figure out where the other could have hidden the documents which could have given him information on the goods carried by the Wells Fargo stages. Not that evidence such as that would be sufficient to incriminate the other in front of a circuit judge, but it could be used to make Barton talk, especially if backed up by a few other facts.

He was on the point of making a second search, confident that he had missed something, when he heard the sound of heavy footsteps coming along the boardwalk outside. Swiftly, he snuffed out the lamp and backed away into one corner of the room. If anyone came into the office, he was relying on them being momentarily unable to see clearly in the pitch darkness. Even a few seconds would be enough for him to take the initiative.

There was the sound of a key being inserted into the lock, metal turning on metal, and then the door leading on to the street was pushed open and a dark figure came into the room. From the other's unsteady gait, he reasoned that he had been drinking. So much the better. Gently, Dan eased himself forward, his right hand closing over the butt of his gun.

The man lurched into the middle of the room, fell against the edge of the table and muttered a harsh curse under his breath as his fingers fumbled for the sulphur matches. As he scraped one along the side of the box and lit the lamp, Dan stepped forward out of the shadows, the gun levelled on the other's chest.

'Surprised to see me, Barton,' he said quietly, watching the other carefully. In his present condition, the sheriff might be tempted to go for his gun, even though he knew it would be sheer suicide to do so. But Barton merely sank down into the chair at the back of his desk and kept his half-closed eyes on Dan as the other walked forward, circled the table, and closed the door softly, locking it with the key which the other had left in the lock.

'Now we can talk without any interruptions,' said Dan smoothly. He went over and sat nonchalantly on the edge of the table, the barrel of the gun pointing at a spot between the other's eyes.

'Just what is the meaning of this, Trafford?' demanded the other hotly. 'Have you gone plumb loco? Drawing a gun on a sheriff.'

'Let's say that I've got good reasons to do this. Seems you've been mixed up in some crooked business, Sheriff. There's a lot of information that points to you being mixed in with the Carrons.'

The other half-lifted himself to his feet, then jerked his body back again, arms held out rigidly in front of him on the table, the light of the lamp throwing his face into shadow. Some of the glazed look had vanished from his eyes and they were narrowed now, filled with an animal cunning. Dan tightened his finger slightly on the trigger.

'You don't deny it then, Sheriff,' he said softly, ominously. It was more of a statement than a question.

'I don't have to answer anything to you, Trafford,' snarled the other sharply. 'These accusations are going to get you nowhere. You can't come in here, breaking into my office after dark, and accuse me of being in league with that gang of outlaws.' Rage and another emotion which Dan couldn't identify struggled for supremacy in his tone. His voice rose slightly in pitch as he went on quickly. 'And why are you here in my office, anyway?' His gaze flicked to Dan's right, not towards the walls, but to the floor in the corner of the room.

Dan straightened slightly. 'So that's where you have everything hidden,' he murmured. 'I never thought of looking there.'

'I don't know what you're talking about, Trafford, Now are you going to get out of here or do I have to arrest you for breaking in? I'm prepared to overlook it this time. but if you don't go, I'll—'

'Just sit there and keep quiet, Sheriff,' snapped Dan tautly. He got to his feet and backed across the room, keeping one eye on the sheriff, ready for him if he decided to go for his gun and fight it out. With his heel, he stamped on the wooden floor in the corner, gave a satisfied nod as his foot hit a hollow spot. 'All right, Sheriff. Over here – and quickly!' For a moment, he thought that the other intended to refuse, but after a moment, Barton struggled to his feet with a sudden oath and walked forward, still swaying a little, but on balance once more, his cunning, agile brain scheming desperately for a way to get out of this position, to turn the tables on Dan.

'You'll regret this, Trafford,' he said hoarsely. 'I'll personally see to it that you're arrested and brought to trial for this. And it won't help you to go running back to Shannon City and looking to your friend Bateson to help you out.'

'I'll risk that,' snapped Dan, pointing with the barrel of the gun towards the floor in the corner of the room. 'Take up those floorboards and we'll take a look-see at what you've got stached away underneath.'

'There's nothing there, Trafford,' snarled the other. His face was working, his lips twisted into a grimace of pure hatred. 'Either you're drunk or you don't know what you're doing.'

'I know what I'm doing all right,' said Dan tightly. 'I'm exposing a murderer, a thief and a treacherous snake who's working hand-in-glove with that outlaw gang, giving them the information they need on what's being carried on the stage. You were the one who told them that we intended to raid their hide-out that night and you were with Luke Carron when he busted his brother out of the jail over at Shannon City. Unfortunately for you, you were seen at the Stacey ranch when you went over there with the Carron brothers.'

'That's a g'damned lie! I was never anywhere near that house when—'

'Just get those floorboards up.' Dan made an ominous motion with the gun and saw the sweat pop out on the other's forehead. He seemed to realize for the first time that if he made the wrong move, he would be shot just as readily as if it were one of the Carrons on the end of that steady gun. Bending, he worked his fingers in at the side of one of the boards, pulled with all of his strength. The board creaked and then snapped upwards, uncovering a strip of the floor.

'Now the next one,' said Dan, 'and then bring over the lamp and we'll take a look-see down that hole.'

'You're going to regret this,' hissed the other as he pulled the second board loose, then got slowly to his feet, eyes narrowed, and walked towards the table, picking up the lamp. Without warning, he turned abruptly, hurled the lamp across the room at Dan. Even though he had expected the other to make a move like that, the suddenness of it took him by surprise. Ducking swiftly, he heard the lamp strike the wall behind him, smash against the brickwork and fall to the floor. If the sheriff had been hoping for the oil to burst into flame and destroy any evidence there might be under the floor, he was doomed to disappointment. By some miracle the spilled oil did not ignite, and the room was plunged into darkness.

Pushing himself up on to his hands and knees, Dan heard the other trying the door, twisting the handle swiftly, urgently. Then, realizing that he could not escape that way, the sheriff turned and began to run across the room, towards the corridor leading past the cells to the rear of the building. Not wishing to use the gun and alarm the neighbourhood, Dan hurled himself forward, hitting the other in the pit of the stomach with his head, like a battering ram. The other gave a sharp gasp of agony as all of the wind was driven from his body by the vicious force of the blow. He stumbled against the wall, then fell sideways over the table. But even as he fell, his hand was clawing for the gun at his side. Reversing his own, Dan tried to use it as a club, but in the darkness with the other squirming like a fish across the table, the butt merely struck the other a glancing blow on the shoulder, causing him to drop his own gun, but doing little other damage.

Savagely, Barton brought up his knee into the pit of Dan's stomach and he twisted back as a stab of agony burst through him. Desperately, the other lunged forward, pushing with his feet against the table. It fell over but there had been sufficient impetus behind the thrust for him to fall on top of Dan, knocking him to the floor with the whole of his weight behind the blow. Dan felt the gun being kicked from his fingers and heard it go sliding into the far corner of the room.

Now it was to be a fight to the finish with bare hands. Barton was fighting for his life. He must have known by now that Dan knew the dirty game he had been playing while in office, that he had been hiding behind the badge of sheriff, all the time working with the outlaws. If the news leaked out, the people of the town would soon see to it that a new sheriff was elected to take his place and he would swing for his complicity in the murder and robbery which the Carron gang had committed over the past months.

Dan fought savagely but scientifically. While the other was trying viciously to gouge out his eyes, he pummelled the other about the stomach with all of the strength of his arms, throwing short jabs to the sheriff's soft underbelly. The other was by far the heavier man, but he was out of condition. He had sat in the office too long to be in proper trim and gradually the pace began to tell on him.

Gasping and hissing for breath, he fell back as Dan got his feet under him and threw the other off. There was a dull, sickening thud as the sheriff's head struck the leg of the table and before he could recover his dazed senses, Dan chopped a swift blow to the tip of his jaw, judging the distance nicely even in the pitch blackness. It was the *coup de grace* as far as Sheriff Barton was concerned. He fell back on to the floor, breathing in harsh gasps. Getting to his feet, Dan went over and retrieved his gun from the corner of the room where it had fallen and pushed it into his holster. There was little to fear from the sheriff now and hunting through a cupboard against one wall, he located another lamp, placed it on the desk and lit it. Filling a jug from the tap in the corner, he threw the cold water over the other's face. Spluttering, the other pushed himself up on to his hands, shaking his head from side to side. Then he opened his eyes and stared up at the stern face which looked down at him.

'You've just come to the end of the trail, Sheriff,' said Dan tightly. 'You've made your last act of mockery of the law. I'm taking you in for complicity in the murder of three Wells Fargo men and for a number of stage robberies. And don't think I can't make those charges stick.'

'You're bluffing, Trafford. You've got no authority to hold me.'

'No?' said the other quietly. 'Reckon when we get back to Shannon City you'll find out differently. But first we'll collect what I came here for.'

Still keeping a wary eye on the other, he went back into the corner of the room, reached down into the hold in the floorboards, felt his fingers close around a bundle of papers and drew them out into the light. The look on the sheriff's face told him more than words that he had hit paydirt.

'I guess there's enough here to satisfy a judge and jury,' he said quietly. 'The contents of every strongbox that left here for Shannon City or the east. Once the Carron gang knew of these, they could be certain of holding up the right stage.'

'Now see here, Trafford. I don't know where you fit into this deal at all. The last I heard you were riding with the Carron gang yourself, and then you suddenly decided to turn them in. Could be you thought you could handle things a lot better yourself. If so, then I'm with you on that. We don't need either Luke or Jeb Carron. With the information I can get, without attracting any attention here in Carson, we could make plenty for ourselves and we need only split it two ways. A third for me, if you like, and the rest for you. What do you say to that proposition?'

Dan shook his head slowly. 'You're even a bigger rat than I took you for, Barton. Now that the game's up, you're still prepared to sell out your friends so long as you can save your own miserable hide.'

'Don't be a fool, Trafford. What have you got to lose? I could get word through to Luke and Jeb, and inside a couple of hours, we could lay an ambush along the trail and that would be the finish of them. Then it would be just you and I. We could run this territory between us.'

'You never give up, do you, Barton?' Dan stuffed the papers into his shirt. 'Now here are the keys. Unlock that street door and walk out quietly. Don't make any funny moves or I'll shoot you in the back. I'm taking you back to Shannon City with me. I've an idea Sheriff Bateson would like to ask you a few questions.'

He tossed the keys to the other, waited until Barton had picked them up then prodded him towards the door. They had almost reached it when Dan heard the sudden noise behind them. He whirled sharply, but not quickly enough.

'Drop that gun, mister, and raise your hands slowly over your head.'

Dan cursed himself mentally for not having remembered that someone might happen along and spot that open window at the back of the building. He allowed the gun to drop from his fingers. It hit the floor with a metallic clatter and Barton whirled swiftly, stooped to pick it up. There was a triumphant grin on his features as he faced Dan.

'Seems you were just in time, Hank,' he said thickly. 'Caught this *hombre* rifling my desk, but he got the drop on me. He's probably in with that Carron gang, they reckoned there was a third man working with them who hadn't been identified. Ever seen this *hombre* before?'

Dan turned and stared at the man who had just come into the room. He wore a deputy's badge on his shirt and he held a long-barrelled Colt in his right hand. He shook his head as he studied Dan's face in the lamplight.

'Nope, Sheriff. Never set eyes on him before. He's new around here. If'n I'd seen him, I'd have remembered him.'

Barton was completely on balance now. He rubbed the side of his mouth where a thin trickle of blood was oozing

94

down his face. His eyes narrowed and his lips drew back into a thin, vicious line across the middle of his face. 'I'm going to show you how we deal with *hombres* like you in Carson,' he said in a low hiss. 'Before I get Hank here to lock you up, you're going to give those papers you stole back to me.'

Before Dan knew what the other intended to do, Barton had drawn back his bunched fist and struck him full on the mouth. He staggered back against the corner of the table, pain jarring along his left arm where the bushwhacker's bullet had glanced off the bone a few hours earlier. Unable to make a move with the deputy's gun on him, he was forced to lean there while Barton took away the incriminating evidence from his shirt.

'You're making a big mistake, Deputy,' said Dan tightly. 'Those papers that Barton has just taken prove his guilt, they show that he's in with the Carron gang, that he's the man who's been supplying them with all of that information which told them which stages to rob and when to keep clear because a posse was riding with the coach.'

'Why don't you quit lying, *hombre*,' said Barton softly, walking back to the desk and pushing the papers inside the drawer. 'It isn't going to help you one little bit. The very fact that you're here, and that you came in through that open window at the back is sufficient evidence. What do you say, Hank?'

'Looks like you caught him red-handed, Sheriff,' said the deputy with a harsh laugh. He moved forward and prodded Dan viciously with the barrel of his gun. 'We ain't got no time for people like you in Carson. What do I do with him, Sheriff, lock him up in the cells for the night?'

'Yeah. In the morning, I've got plans for him. Reckon he'll think twice about trying to rob the Sheriff after that.'

He laughed thinly and the deputy joined in as he herded Dan along the narrow corridor towards the cells.

'Inside.' The deputy held the door open and motioned Dan to go inside. His other gun had been taken away from him, as had the long-bladed knife which he carried concealed along his wrist. It was useless to argue with these men. The deputy was only doing his duty as he saw it. There was little doubt that he was an honest man, but he would sooner believe the sheriff than a man who had clearly broken into the building and had taken papers from the sheriff.

'When do I get to see a lawyer?' said Dan harshly, as the other closed the door on him and turned the key in the lock.'

'There ain't no lawyers in this town for people like you,' said the other. He turned on his heel and walked away leaving the place in darkness.

CHAPTER FIVE

JAILBREAK!

DAN Trafford sat on the edge of the narrow bunk and stared morosely in front of him. He had fallen into a trap of his own making and there was no one to blame but himself, and still the feeling of angry chagrin remained in his mind. After a while, he got to his feet and moved slowly around the cell, feeling the walls and examining the window closely, but the steel bars set in the stonework were strong and unyielding, though rusted. No way out through there, he decided; and now that he was behind bars, Barton would make sure that he never got out. Once Dan was free, it would spell the end for the sheriff of Carson.

Frustrated, he lowered himself on to the bunk again, leaned back and clasped his hands at the back of his head, staring at the dim ceiling. It was possible that if he didn't turn up at Shannon City the following day, Bateson would realize that something was wrong, and come looking for him and although he had little real jurisdiction outside his own territory, he would make sure that he was released on this trumped up charge even if he had to go to the extent of breaking his earlier promise and showing the Ranger's badge. But the faint hope in his mind died almost before it was born. If he knew Barton, the crooked sheriff would have him out of the jail and tucked away somewhere where no one could find him, until the Carron brothers had looked him over and decided what to do with him. The prospect was not encouraging. Stretching himself out on the hard bunk, he tried to think things out. He doubted whether Barton would try to smuggle him out of the jail that night. It would mean trying to square things with the deputy who had caught him on the wrong foot.

Once on a stage eastward bound, away from Carson, it would be easy for a hold-up to be arranged, and he would be taken off into the desert where some prospector might stumble across his bones in a future year. In the distance, at the end of the passage he could hear voices, but they were too low for him to be able to make out the words. Sheriff Barton and the deputy, he reasoned, possibly discussing what they would do with him.

He tried to pick out an odd word or two, but when he found this to be impossible, he gave it up, turned over on to his side, pulled the thin blanket over and closed his eyes. He fell into a troubled sleep from which he woke to find the sunlight streaming through the small barred window over his head and the deputy on the point of unlocking the door.

'All right, wake up, fella,' said the other. He held his gun in one hand and the shallow metal tray in the other. 'Just stay where you are and you won't git hurt. My orders are to feed you and keep an eye on you.'

'You know where the sheriff is right now?'

The other looked at him sharply, then gave a brief nod, suspecting nothing. 'Sure, mister. He headed out around dawn. Seemed in a hurry.'

'I guess he would be,' nodded Dan. He eyed the food on the plate with a look of distaste, but the hunger in his stomach got the better of his feelings and be began to eat. The deputy stood close to the door, evidently reluctant to leave. Dan had him figured for a simple type of man. Honest, but dull-witted. He would obey orders to the letter, no matter who gave them, even to the extent of shooting him if he tried to make a break for it.

'You reckon you know where he's gone?' Surprise

98

showed on the man's face.

'You'd never believe me if I told you where.' Dan spooned the food into his mouth. Although he showed no sign of noticing, he knew that the deputy was watching him more closely, evidently unable to understand him.

'What would you say if I told you that Sheriff Barton was working with the Carron gang, that he's been feeding them information so's they could rob the stages on the way to Shannon City, that I've been working for Sheriff Bateson there?'

'I'd say you was just trying to talk your way outa jail,' grinned the other. 'The sheriff told me everything about you last night. Shucks, it don't seem right to hang a man on just that evidence.'

'So they figure on hanging me, do they'?' Dan nodded, apparently unconcerned. 'Reckon they'll have to do it pretty soon. Once Sheriff Bateson learns that I'm here he'll be over with a posse and plenty of evidence that Barton is the guilty party. Then you're going to look foolish, aren't you?'

From beneath lowered lids he knew that his words had struck home. The other was now unsure of him, was beginning to doubt. He pressed home with his advantage. 'I'll bet the sheriff didn't let you get a look at those papers he pushed so hurriedly into his desk last night.'

'Why should he do that?' The other pushed himself upright from the door and stared challengingly at him.

'Because those papers would have cleared me of the charges he made last night. Sure I broke into the office. I had to get my hands on that evidence which would put him where he belongs, show conclusively that he's mixed up with the Carron gang. He even admitted so much just before you burst in on us. But with me locked away inside this jail, he knows he's safe. I'm the only one who can testify against him.'

'You'll git the chance to tell all this to the jury when they bring you to trial, mister. I can testify to the fact that he had some papers in his hand when I took you back to the cells and that you had them tucked away inside your shirt.'

Dan grinned mirthlessly. 'You're very simple. D'you think for one minute that I'll ever get a trial? Barton knows that if I get in front of a jury, I'll spill everything I know. There'll be a stage waiting to take me out of town some time today, once he gets back from his meeting with the Carron brothers and I can assure you I'll never reach the end of that journey. There'll be a couple of men waiting somewhere along the trail and I'll be taken into the desert and shot. You see, I know too much for their safety.'

'Now you ain't talkin' sense at all, mister. It ain't going to be like that at all. You'll get a fair trial, I promise you.'

'I'm afraid it's going to be taken out of your hands. You're just the deputy here. Sheriff Barton will give the orders, and they'll have been passed down from his boss, Luke Carron.'

'Look, mister,' protested the other harshly, 'I don't know what this is all about. I've been given my orders and I've got to hold you here until I get word from the sheriff.'

Dan shrugged, 'Suit yourself.' He pushed the empty plate away from him, then lifted his head and said quietly. 'Don't I get anything to drink in this jail?'

'Huh, oh sure. I'll git you somethin'.' The other picked up the empty plate, still keeping a wary eye on him, the gun in his right hand covering every move Dan made. He locked the door behind him as he moved back along the passage. Dan lay back on the hunk, his mind working like greased lightning in his head. How long before the sheriff got back from his meeting with the Carrons? If he had ridden out around dawn, he would make good time to wherever they were hiding. He twisted his lips into a grim smile. There was no doubt what the orders would be that the Carron brothers would give him. Whatever happened, the sheriff would not be able to shoot him out of hand, no matter how dangerous he was. That pleasure was to be reserved for either Jeb or Luke. But they wouldn't want him held in the jail for long. Barton would be told to get him out of Carson and along the trail leading east as soon as possible.

He rose to his feet as he heard the deputy coming back. The man held a mug of something hot in his hand. This time, he made no attempt to open the door, but pushed it through the bars. 'This is the best I could get for you, mister.'

Dan took it, knowing that there would be no chance of throwing it in the other's face as he had intended if the deputy had opened the door and stepped inside the cell. He forced himself to relax and it was at that moment that there was a sudden commotion in the room outside and he heard a woman's loud and familiar voice calling:

'All right, Hank; where are you hiding now?'

Dan almost laughed at the expression on the deputy's face. He said quietly: 'Reckon you'd better go see what the lady wants, she seems to be mighty steamed up about something.'

The other gave a quick nod and hurried off along the passage. Dan did not have long to wait. The man was back in a few moments, and behind him came the large and unmistakable figure of Kitty Masters. Dan had never been so glad to see anyone in his life. She gave the deputy a sharp push that sent him staggering against the bars of the cell. 'Now get that door open and let him out, d'you hear me, otherwise I'm going to get mad. And then you'll regret it.'

'Yes, Miss Kitty.' He fumbled with the lock of the cell, then twisted the key, opened the door and stood to one side as Dan stepped out. 'I'm only obeying orders, you know.'

'Sure, you always obey orders, don't you. Well this time, I'm giving them.' She turned to Dan. 'How've they been treating you in this pig-sty, Dan? I figured you might need a little help, so I decided to come on into Carson and see how things were going.'

'Believe me, Kitty, I'm mighty glad that you did. But there's a lot we have to do and very little time. Things have

101

been moving fast since I left you yesterday, but I'll explain on the way back to Shannon City. In the meantime, what do we do with this *hombre?*'

'Reckon he'd look better in his own jail, Dan,' drawled the other. She reached forward and pulled the deputy's gun from its holster, then nodded towards the open door of the cell. 'Better get inside, Hank, while I'm still feeling patient.'

'Now see here, Miss Kitty, you can't do this thing to me. When Sheriff Barton gits back, there's going to be hell to pay.'

'Reckon you'll have plenty of time to think over what you're going to say to him when he does get back,' said Dan, grinning widely. He closed the door on the other, locked it and threw the bunch of keys along the passage. 'I guess he'll let you out when he gets back.' He paused, then went on quietly: 'On the other hand, he may be so mad that you didn't keep me here that he'll let you stay in that cell for the rest of your life.'

'For pity's sake, mister, if you're going to head outa town, at least take me with you., I'd sooner be on the run than face Barton when he finds out what's happened.' He turned to Kitty Masters. 'You got me into this, Kitty. Let me out of here and I'll swear I never saw you.'

She shook her head. 'Nothing doing Hank. You're in there now and there you'll stay until your boss gets back. But when he does, tell him this from the both of us: he'd better get out of town quick, because when we come back, there's going to be a showdown and he'll be on the wrong end of a gun.'

She followed Dan along the passage, out through the Sheriff's office at the end. Inside the office, Dan paused, moved quickly to the drawer in the desk and pulled if open. It was empty. He looked up and shrugged.

'Was there something important in that drawer, Dan?' she asked, watching him from the open doorway.

'The evidence that I found last night. Barton put it there when the deputy took me along the passage to the cell. I guess it was only a faint hope that he might have left it there. My guess is that he must have taken it with him to Luke Carron. They'll have destroyed it by now.'

'Don't let it get you down, Dan, there'll be a lot more evidence against them before we're through. We'll hang them yet, if they don't die with a bullet in their crooked hearts.'

Outside, there was a buckboard waiting with a pair of high-spirited horses in the shafts. 'They'll have taken your horse by now, Dan,' she said as she saw him looking up and down the dusty street. 'Get in and we'll head out to Shannon City, before more trouble arrives in Carson. Barton won't be long getting back here and when he finds you're gone, there'll be a posse on our tail within a few minutes.'

Dan slipped on to the buckboard beside her, whipped up the horses. Seconds later, they were driving down the main street of Carson, heading west. As he drove, Dan tried to hoard the strength of the two horses. Evidently Kitty had ridden them hard on her way into Carson. If they were to put plenty of distance between themselves and any pursuit, it wouldn't do to tire out both horses quickly while they were still some miles from Shannon City and help.

'What made you come looking for me, Kitty?' he asked quietly, not taking his eyes off the rolling country, on the sides of the winding trail.

She shrugged non-committally. 'I had a talk with Mary Stacey. She told me about that attempt to bushwhack you in the street yesterday and I figured that they would have another try. My mind wouldn't let me rest this morning – early – and when you weren't back by sun-up, I knew that something was wrong. What happened – did they surprise you in the sheriff's office?'

Briefly, Dan outlined to her everything that had happened after he had got into the office. She listened intently, then nodded. 'I guessed as much. That deputy – Hank – he's a good man, but slow and simple. I've known him for many years now. He'd have shot you down if you'd

103

tried to escape by yourself, you know that?'

'I thought he might. That's why I was so glad to see you there.' He bit his lower lip. There were still a lot of unanswered questions running through his mind and it was difficult, at that moment, to know which was the most urgent and important. 'I suppose Mary told you why she wanted to see me. Do you know what those outlaws could have on her father to force him to help them?'

'Nothing that could be as important as that. He's a big and influential man around here, owns the biggest spread. It could be something to do with his past, before he came here, but that's all I can tell you.'

'I wonder if it was anything to do with the war?' mused Dan quietly,

'Why do you say that?' She arched her brows interrogatively.

'It might make sense. They were all in the army together. Luke Carron was an officer with the South and it's possible that Stacey was with the same outfit.'

'If there is anything, then I'll stake my reputation – for what it's worth – that he was framed by those outlaws. He's a straight, upright man. I'll swear to that, and there ain't nobody going to make me change my mind about Bob Stacey.'

'You're a good friend, Kitty,' he said, grinning. By, now, they were less than three miles from the outskirts of Shannon City and throwing an occasional glance over his shoulder, Dan felt confident that they were not being pursued. It was just possible that Sheriff Barton and the two Carron brothers had had more to talk about than he had imagined and with the deputy locked away safely, inside the cell, it might be several hours before his escape was noticed.

But they weren't that lucky. As they began to climb among the trees, he caught sight of the cloud of dust behind them far out over the open prairie. The riders, not yet visible through the dust cloud thrown up by their horses, were cutting in on them at an angle to the trail and he guessed that they were moving across country in the hope of heading them off before they got to Shannon City. With a wild yell, he whipped the two horses, urging them forward. The buckboard swayed and lurched dangerously on the uneven surface of the trail and beside him, Kitty Masters hung on to the side with both hands. But once, when he glanced at her face out of the corner of his eye to see how she was taking it, he was surprised to see that there was no fear or apprehension on her features. Rather there was a look of grim determination and something almost akin to exhilaration as if she were enjoying every minute of this desperate dash to freedom.

He cursed a little under his breath as he saw that the pursuers were gradually diminishing the distance between them and he knew, by a swift calculation, that they would catch up with them before they had a chance of riding into Shannon City.

'Can't imagine how they got started so soon,' he said harshly, 'it means that our getaway must have been noticed just after we left. They've been circling around us, possibly hoping to lull us into a state of false security'

By now the sun was high overhead and there were few shadows across the trail of the surrounding country. He knew with a sudden certainty that they had been seen, even at that distance.

'They're sure burning up ground,' muttered Kitty thinly. 'Can't you get any more out of the horses?'

He shook his head savagely. 'They're just about finished. That hard ride into Carson and then the drive back has taken a lot out of them. Those horses behind us are fresh, you can stake your life on that. They'll catch up with us about a mile further on. You'd better keep your head down when they get a little closer. There's likely to be lead flying.'

'I'm not afraid of a little shooting, Dan.' She dug into the back of the buckboard, came up with a long-barrelled Lee-Enfield. With a faint sense of surprise, Dan noticed that it was a new gun and from the way in which the woman handled it, she knew how to use it to the best advantage.

'No need to start firing yet,' he warned. 'They're still well out of range. Think you can use that gun?'

She nodded shortly. 'Been using one of these ever since I was a kid back in Kansas. Then you never knew when it would come in handy. I reckon those owlhoots back there will get the biggest surprise of their lives when they get a little closer.'

'I'm sure they will,' said Dan with feeling. The horses strained as they pulled the buckboard along the trail which still wound upwards along a rocky ledge. Down below, in the wide stretching valley, the riders could be clearly seen now. He estimated that there were close on a dozen of them, a posse raised either by Barton or the deputy. They would not dare to shoot them down once they hit the streets of Shannon City, but there were still two miles to go yet and he knew they would never make it in time.

When the riders were less than a quarter of a mile away to their right, he leaned over and shouted at the top of his voice: 'All right, Kitty. Let them have it now. I'll try to hold the buckboard steady.' He knew that, much as he would have liked to take the gun from her and give her the reins, that the horses were now pulling and swerving too much for her to hope to hold them steady, and the first wrong move could be enough to send them hurtling over the steep side of the trail, down among the rocks some thirty feet below.

Beside him, Kitty Masters began firing. Out of the corner of his eye, he saw one of the leading men slide out of the saddle and hit the dust, his body rolling over and over several times before coming to rest. He did not move after that and his mount plunged on riderless, running in front of the main body of horsemen and throwing them into some confusion. But it was only a temporary respite. They soon regained their balance and came driving forward, scattering a little into a wide line as they swung around the side of the trail, evidently making their move to cut them off. Dan threw a swiftly apprehensive eye ahead of them. It was only a matter of minutes now before the first of those men reached the trail about five hundred yards ahead, made their way across it and began firing directly at them.

Gritting his teeth, he pulled the gun from its holster, holding the reins in his right hand with all the strength he could muster, firing swiftly and savagely with his left. The stiffness in his injured arm was temporarily forgotten now as he saw two men topple from their mounts as the bullets hit them. Several of the riders were throwing lead now, ignoring the fact that there was a woman with him, and he heard several bullets hum dangerously close to his head.

With only seconds to spare, they drove past the men moving in from the side. Ahead of them, the trail wound downwards now, moving between the tall, sky-rearing pines. Twenty yards further on, it turned sharply and as the horses plunged and reared, he eased the buckboard around the sharply-angled bend. It was then that he saw it. From further back along the trail, it had been hidden by the bend and the trees. The thick trunk of the tree lay, directly across the trail, blocking it almost completely. There was no way around it, even if he had had time in which to turn the horses. Desperately, he pulled on the reins. Even as he did so, there was the burst of gunfire from the other side of the fallen tree and he knew that he had ridden straight into a trap.

The horses reared and threatened to stampede. With all of his strength, he pulled on the reins and before the buckboard had ground to a halt, he had seized the woman and pulled her off, one arm around her waist as he hurried her towards the trees and the thick underbrush on the side of the trail. Bullets zipped and hummed like a swarm of angry locusts around their heads as they dropped down into the bushes, the long thorns tearing the backs of their hands and arms. A swift glance told him that Kitty had somehow managed to retain her grip on the rifle and even as he looked back along the road, the thunder of the approaching riders in his ears, she had whipped up the gun and snapped a shot at a head which appeared briefly, above the trunk of the tree. The man's hat went flying and he pulled his head in like the horns of a salted snail.

'Good shooting, Kitty,' he said warmly. 'But we don't seem to stand much of a chance holed up here. No sense in trying to go back the way we came. There are close on twelve or fifteen men there, acting on Barton's orders, And those two coyotes crouched down behind that tree are the Carron brothers. I'd recognize them anywhere. They must have figured this is the way we'd come if I managed to get out of that jail.'

He looked about him wildly for an avenue of escape, but to have gone deeper into the trees would have meant that they would be vulnerable to attack from all sides and with so many men ranged against them, they wouldn't remain free for more than a few minutes. Had he been alone, he would have tried to slither away through the brush and slip through their lines before they had a chance to consolidate their position. But with Kitty with him, that was completely out of the question.

The woman seemed to have divined his thoughts, for she turned suddenly and said sharply and seriously: 'I can hold them off here Dan, long enough for you to get away through the trees back there. It's you they're after. They won't harm me even if they manage to get me.'

He shook his head vehemently. 'Don't talk that way, Kitty. I can't leave you here. You've no idea what the Carron brothers would do to you if they discovered that I'd slipped through their fingers again. Those two men are inhuman fiends. They'd think nothing of torturing a woman and then shooting her out of hand.'

'Then what do we do, Dan? We can't stay here for long. They'll start closing in on us from all sides and pretty soon we're going to run out of ammunition. Then what do we fight them with?'

Dan's eyes narrowed. They were in a tight spot; but even so, there had to be some way out for them. They were so close to Shannon City that it would be a terrible trick of fate if they were to lose out now. He debated whether or not to turn himself over to the posse. At least, he doubted if they would hand him over to the Carrons. Barton was probably there with them, it was true, and he might shoot them out of hand if the outlaws did not want to show themselves.

Two men came snaking through the trees to their right. He did not recognize them and knew they were men from Carson, sworn in as deputies by Barton, He did not want to shoot these men who were, after all, merely doing their duty. With a cool deliberateness, he fired a couple of shots, sufficiently close to their heads to cause them to pull back quickly. He doubted if they would come within killing distance again.

'Pretty soon, they're going to pluck up enough courage to try to rush us,' he said tightly, through thinned lips. 'I don't like the idea of killing those men from Carson. All I want to do is to get the Carron brothers and that crooked sheriff in my sights. But with so many men with them, they'll stay in the background and leave the dirty work to them.'

Even as he spoke, he heard Luke Carron's voice from behind the tree blocking the road: 'You over there, Sheriff Barton?'

A moment later, Barton's voice called back from somewhere among the trees: 'Yeah, I'm here. What is it?'

'Trafford's in there somewhere, Sheriff. We saw him headed this way and felled the tree to stop him. I want him alive. As for the woman who's with him, you can take her any way you like, dead or alive. She ought to know what the sentence is for abetting a wanted criminal.'

'That's a fine sentiment coming from someone like you, Carron,' yelled Dan loudly. He hoped that some of the posse might hear the words and realize just who was

109

behind that tree.

'You're making a mistake, Trafford.' Carron's voice was punctuated by a shot which hummed into the undergrowth close to his shoulder. 'My name isn't Carron. I'm the new Wells Fargo agent sent here to look into these stage robberies. I guess we've got our man holed up right now; what do you say fellas?'

Dan tightened his lips. So that was the line that Carron was taking. He knew that none of the posse would have seen the outlaw's face and Barton would have briefed them well on the way there.

'Listen to me, Trafford,' called Barton's voice a moment later. 'You two give yourselves up and we'll take you in to jail back in Carson. If you're innocent of the charges against you, you'll git a fair trial. If we got to surround you and take you the hard way, mebbe we won't bother about taking you alive at all. I've got the lives of my men to think of.'

'Why don't you and those two Carrons come in and get me,' roared Dan loudly.

'We will.' There was an ominous note in the other's voice and Dan guessed that Barton was rapidly running out of patience. There was a rustling in the trees a little distance away and he guessed that the rest of the men were moving forward quickly, determined to get it over with as soon as possible. Only the fact that Carron wanted him taken alive, must have held them in check so far. The movement among the trees was clearly audible now. It seemed to come from all around them, but he knew that Jeb and Luke Carron were still crouched behind that tree. It was essential that they should not show themselves to the men of the posse, and yet they had to prevent him from moving back along the trail,

Carefully, Dan refilled the chambers of his guns from the bullets in his belt. Another handful after those had been fired and that would be all. He glanced at Kitty Master, saw the firm set of her mouth. 'Sorry I got you into this, Kitty. Guess there's not much chance of us getting out of this alive. Too many of them against us and when they start moving in we—'

He broke off suddenly. In the distance, there was a new sound. The drumming of hooves on the trail. Swiftly, he jerked his head upright, unable to believe his ears, then knew that he had been right from the beginning. Those horses were being ridden hard and they were approaching from the direction of Shannon City. Seconds later, he saw the two dark figures rising up from behind the fallen tree, darting through the undergrowth towards the far side of the trail. Swiftly, he snapped a couple of shots after them, but none of them hit and after a few moments, there was the sound of horses being driven hard towards the open prairie beyond the trail.

Cursing softly under his breath, he got to his feet just as the leading riders from Shannon City came into sight beyond the fallen tree. He recognized Bateson with them. The sheriff slid swiftly from his mount, clambered over the tree and came forward quickly. As Dan came into the open, on the trail, he was aware of the posse from Carson moving out of the undergrowth, their guns drawn and fixed on him but none of them made any attempt to open fire. There was no sign of Sheriff Barton, and he guessed that the crooked lawman had slipped away the minute he knew that the game was up.

'The Carron brothers,' said Dan swiftly. 'They've just lit out for the prairie and if you get a handful of men after them you might stand a chance of finding their trail.'

Bateson yelled a couple of orders to the men still astride their mounts on the far side of the tree and they turned swiftly and rode off to the north. It was doubtful if they would catch up with the two outlaws, thought Dan inwardly, but they might be able to trail them for some distance, far enough to tell whether they had doubled back on their trail and were heading south again towards the old mine workings.

'You know this man, Sheriff?' asked Hank, the deputy. He came forward and viewed Dan with suspicion. 'He broke outa jail in Carson this morning, with the help of Miss Masters.'

'Sure, I know him,' nodded Bateson. 'He's been working for me for some time now. We'd an idea that Sheriff Barton was mixed up with the Carrons and I sent him into Carson to look for evidence that we could pin on that crooked lawman. Since I've no jurisdiction there, I couldn't do much myself and it was essential that we didn't warn Barton of our suspicions.'

'Sheriff Barton in with the Carrons.' There was surprise and incredulity in the deputy's tone. 'But that's impossible. Why only this morning he—' He broke off and glanced about him quickly, eyes scanning the faces of the men standing around him. 'Anybody here seen the sheriff. I figure he ought to answer these charges himself and if he can't—'

'Don't worry, he can't,' broke in Dan thinly. 'For the simple reason that he's no longer here. He slipped out as soon as he saw that there was no chance of either killing me or taking me alive. He knew that Sheriff Bateson here could clear me of those charges he made last night, and also implicate him with those outlaws. Now he's gone to join them.'

'No point in sending any more of my men after them,' said Bateson quietly. He glanced in the direction of the valley which stretched away to the north. 'They'd never catch up with them now. Those horses would be fresh and they've got too much of a start. Best thing we can do now, Dan, is get that tree moved and then ride into town. I suggest that the rest of you men ride back to Carson. If Barton shows up there, hold him on suspicion of murder and robbery.'

'All right, Sheriff. Guess I'm convinced.' The deputy went back to his horse and swung himself up in the saddle. A few moments later, the posse rode off along the trail. It was the work of a few moments to hitch a couple of lassos around the trunk, tie them to the saddles of two horses and haul the timber off the trail. Dan climbed up on to the buckboard beside Kitty Masters and they moved off into Shannon City.

'So he did have that evidence,' murmured Bateson, nodding. 'But you think it's been destroyed by now?'

'I'm reasonably certain that it has. Those papers would be too incriminating to be left where anyone could get their hands on them. Either Luke Carron has them or they've been burned. But there was enough there to implicate Barton with the robberies if not with any of the murders committed by the Carron gang.'

'At least we've driven him in with them now. He won't dare show his face in either Shannon City or Carson again. And he won't be able to inform Luke of what we intend to do.'

'Is there another plan hatching inside that scheming mind of yours, Dan'?'

'Mebbe. But first I want to have a talk with Bob Stacey.'

'Stacey? Now what in tarnation can he have to do with this? He's a big man around here, Dan. You'll be lucky if you get on to his spread. He has guards posted around the boundary wire and it's my guess that they have orders to shoot to kill if anyone tries to ride in.'

'I reckon I'll try, just the same,' said Dan quietly, 'There are a few things I want to get straightened out. Then I figure we might be able to lay a trap for the Carrons.'

'You know that they've sworn to kill you, Dan,' said the other soberly. 'I don't know if they have any men with them now, apart from Barton. There are always some cutthroats around these parts willing to join in with any outlaw band. Men who're running away from the law, others who just want easy pickings, the chance to strike it rich without any hard work; and the odd gunslinger who kills just for the sheer sadistic love of it.' He looked down at the sheaf of wanted posters on his desk, fingering through them. 'Quite a handful, aren't they?' he said, glancing up. 'And some of them known to be operating in this territory. I've a feeling that Luke Carron has a very persuasive tongue when it comes to getting men like these to join him. It won't take him long to build up that outlaw band of his again.'

'Then we've got to move fast and see to it that he never gets the chance.' Dan said harshly. He got to his feet, 'Which way is it to Stacey's spread?'

The other stared hard at him for a moment, then shrugged. 'Keep riding along the trail to the west. It's about five miles out. You can't miss it. The trail runs along the southern edge of it. So long as you stay on the trail, you're all right. But if you ride off it, through the boundary wire, then you're taking your life into your hands. He's a powerful man, is Bob Stacey, honest but ruthless. When he gives orders that no strangers are to be allowed on his spread, he sees to it that those orders are carried out.'

'Not a very sociable character, is he?' murmured Dan as he strode towards the door. 'Could be that he's got something to hide. If so, the sooner we know what it is, the better.'

With his own horse back in Carson, he borrowed Bateson's and rode off towards the west, heading out of Shannon City. There was the taut feeling within him that the threatened showdown with the Carron brothers would happen in the very near future. But he had to know where Bob Stacey stood in this deal and he did not try to fool himself on another point too: he also wanted to see Mary Stacey again. Somehow, he had found it difficult to forget about her, even though he had seen her only twice and had known her for only a few days.

He rode slowly along the western trail, through pleasant country, which contrasted starkly with the inhospitable nature of the desert which lay not too far to the south. There had been a few mine workings out on this side of Shannon City, but like those to the south, they had been worked out long before and lay derelict and abandoned. The sun was past its zenith now but still warm with a slight breeze blowing from the north. Giving the horse its head, he relaxed in the saddle, trying to shape things in his mind. The danger that more outlaws and gunhawks might join Luke Carron was a very real one. He kept telling himself that and thought of little else.

Five miles out of town, he came across part of the Stacey spread for the first time. The barbed wire stretched along the edge of the trail, unbroken for the best part of a mile. On the other side of the wire, he saw some of the finest country he had ever seen. The pasture there was lush and green and he recognized instantly that the beef feeding on it were of the best quality. He saw no sign of any herd riders as he made his way slowly along the trail, although he kept his eyes open for the first sign of men on the spread.

Half a mile further on, he came to a wide gate set in the wire. For a moment he paused before it, then thrust it open and rode through, closing it behind him. The large herd he had noticed from the trail lay to the east of him, about a mile away and in front of him, a narrow, well-ridden trail rose up and vanished among the trees on top of a low rise. He spurred his mount towards them. According to Bateson, the ranch-house lay in that direction and the closer he got to it without being shot at, the better chance he had of talking to Stacey alive.

He topped the low rise and reined the horse, sitting tall in the saddle, taking in everything in a quick, sweeping glance. The ranch-house was just visible, down below, about a mile away to the west. There were signs of activity around it and he thought he saw the slim figure of Mary Stacey in the courtyard, but he couldn't be sure from that distance. There were also one or two of the ranch hands down there and as he watched, a small group of them saddled up and rode off to the north. He watched them go, then began to ease the horse dawn the slope. He had gone less than ten yards when a harsh voice behind him said thinly: 'Just stand right where you are, cowboy. One move towards those guns of yourn and you're a dead man.'

Dan stiffened in the saddle, then lifted his hands until

they were clasped over the crown of his hat. Very slowly, he turned his head. The men had come up on him from the far side of the rise, hidden by the trees. They were not on horseback which explained why he had heard nothing. There were five of them, standing in a small group watching him with hostile eyes and they all held rifles trained on him. He knew that even if he did manage to go for his guns, he could not hope to plug all of them before one pulled the trigger of his rifle. At that distance, it would be impossible for them to miss.

'Just what is this?' he asked pleasantly, forcing a puzzled look on to his face. 'I came riding here hoping to have a word with Mister Stacey and the next thing I know there are five rifles trained on me.'

The man who had spoken grinned mirthlessly. 'You ought to know that Mister Stacey don't like strangers trespassing on his spread. Too many of his prime heads of beef have gone amissing lately.'

'Do you figure that if I were a rustler I'd come here alone and in broad daylight?' asked Dan.

'We don't figure anything, mister,' said the other. He lowered the barrel of the rifle slightly. 'Throw down those guns – and fast.'

Dan shrugged, realizing that there was nothing else he could do in the circumstances but obey. Unbuckling his gunbelt he allowed it to slip from his fingers on to the grass. One of the men moved forward carefully and picked it up.

'That's better, cowboy. Only fair to tell you that we have orders to shoot anybody who tries to cross this spread.'

'Why? I ain't done nothing,' he countered. 'All I want is to see Mister Stacey. It's important that I talk with him.'

'Don't worry, you'll see him. We're taking you to him right now. Git down off that horse and follow us. Any funny moves and we'll be taking you in to him – dead. This trigger finger of mine is beginning to get itchy.'

Dan shrugged but said nothing as he slid to the ground. The man who had picked up his gunbelt took hold of the reins and brought the horse along. It was clear that they were taking no chances with him, even though they outnumbered him by five to one. When they reached the ranch-house, there were only a few hands in the courtyard and his captors led him straight to the door at the side, motioning him to go inside. Stepping inside, he found himself in a long, wide corridor and the men herded him along it, not once lowering their rifles.

As he paused in front of the door at the end of the corridor, one of the men stepped forward, around him, and knocked loudly on the panelled wood. There was a pause, then Dan heard a man's voice say something from inside the room and the next moment the man had thrown the door open and he was ushered into the room.

Bob Stacey sat behind a low, polished desk in one corner of the room, overlooking the garden outside. The tall, glass windows were open and the breeze blew into the room.

Dan eyed the other from beneath lowered lids, liking what he saw. Stacey was a man in his early fifties, he guessed, with an open rugged face and piercing grey eyes like those of his daughter. His mouth was firm and showed determination, but also something else; something which showed in his eyes rather than in the cut of his face. Was it a trace of worried fear? wondered Dan inwardly. The look of a man who had something terrible to hide, something he had had to live with for a great many years and who was afraid of every man who came to the spread. It made sense, he decided, as he stood there, looking at the other, feeling the piercing glance of those grey eyes run over him, trying to assess him, trying to figure out why he was there and if he represented any danger to him, or whether he was just another cowpuncher who had strayed on to the spread by accident.

'We caught him riding over at the south end of the spread, boss,' said the man beside Dan. 'He claims he wants to talk with you, so we decided to bring him in. He's unarmed.'

Bob Stacey tightened his lips. 'What were you doing on my ranch?' he asked tightly, in a deep voice. 'Don't you know that I've given orders that all people found trespassing on my property are to be shot?'

'I didn't,' said Dan quietly. 'And even if I had, I would still have taken that chance. What I have to say to you, is private and important.'

The other's brow knit for a moment in perplexity. Dan figured that he was debating within himself whether or not to listen to him, or whether to get rid of him, on the off chance that he was the law and knew something about his tie-in with the Carron gang.

'I can explain my presence here far better if we're alone,' said Dan quietly. He glanced about him at the men who stood in the doorway. 'I think you'll understand why if you'll just give me a chance to talk. I assure you that I am unarmed.'

'OK.' The other gave a brief nod. 'Jake. Take the rest of the boys and remain outside. I'll call if I want you.'

'Very well, Mister Stacey.' The other nodded, threw Dan a quick look and then backed out of the door with the other men, closing it behind him. Dan could hear them moving around in the corridor outside. Then their presence was forgotten as he turned back towards the other.

Bob Stacey leaned back in his chair, took out a cigar, bit the end off it and lit it with a flourish, blowing smoke into the air. But to Dan's trained eye, it was perfectly plain that his air of nonchalant ease was merely an illusion. Deep down inside, the other was as worried as hell, trying to figure out how much he knew and why he had ridden into his place like this, allowing himself to be disarmed and taking the risk of being shot on sight.

'Well, cowboy,' said the other harshly. 'What is it you want to talk about? Whatever it is, it had better be important, otherwise I might still change my mind and turn you over to Jake and the rest of the boys.'

'Perhaps,' smiled Dan faintly. 'First I should mention that I believe you to be an honest and upright man in spite

118

of these threats you've made. But I've had a talk with your daughter and—'

'Mary?' The other's tone was sharp and he got swiftly to his feet, knuckles white as they rested on top of the desk. 'What has she got to do with this? She has only just returned from the east.'

'She's worried about you, Mister Stacey. But perhaps if I tell you who I am, it might help. My name is Trafford.' He saw the look of recognition in the other's eyes at the mere mention of his name. 'Dan Trafford. I'm a United States Ranger and I'm here at the request of Sheriff Bateson of Shannon City, to help in trapping and destroying the Carron gang. At the moment, I don't know what it is they have on you, why you've been forced to help them; but whatever it is, the time has come now, when you'll have to help me; because that's the only way you can redeem yourself in your daughter's eyes.'

CHAPTER SIX

A TIME OF RECKONING

FOR a brief moment, there was anger on the other's face; a look which gave way almost immediately to one of utter defeat. He slumped down into his chair and rested his arms on the desk. 'I suppose Mary told you about all this,' he said in a hushed whisper. 'She must have been the one. Only she could have guessed that anything was wrong. She's been acting strangely ever since she got back here, coming home long before she was supposed to come.'

Dan nodded. 'She told me everything that she suspected and I put two and two together and came up with some answers that I'd like to check with you.'

Bob Stacey sighed, then buried his face in his hands. 'What can I say that would make things any better. So I hid those two outlaws when they came here demanding that I help them. There was nothing else I could do. They've got me over a barrel, Trafford and there's nothing I can figure on doing that will get me free. Good God, if there were, I'd have done it long ago no matter how much it cost.'

'Sometimes, the only way to be free is to face up to trouble, to fight it with everything you've got. I reckoned that the Carrons had something on you, otherwise you'd never have done what they asked. What I'd like to know is: what is it that they know, and what they're holding over your head? Care to tell me?'

The other kept looking down at his hands as if hoping to find the answer to his problems there, then his shoulders slumped again. 'There's nothing you can do, Trafford. Unless you kill those two outlaws. Then I'll be free again.'

'That isn't the way to freedom and you know it. You're a big man around here; at least everybody I've met since I've been here keeps telling me so. Now it's up to you to show how big you are. I need your help if I'm to finish what I came here to do.'

The rancher looked at him in silence for several moments, then nodded heavily. 'Very well, Trafford. I suppose it will help too, to tell it to someone, even though I doubt whether you'll believe me. I've lived with this too long now. I've got to tell it to somebody.'

'Go ahead, I'm listening.' Dan lowered himself into the chair at the side of the desk and waited for the other to begin.

'As you probably know, I fought with the South in the war. I was a Major with a forward scouting unit. Towards the end of the war, we were out on patrol when we met up with a strong force of Union troops. We were hopelessly outnumbered and I decided to pull back before we were spotted. Luke Carron was in my unit at that time. Even then, he had that sadistic streak in him. He wanted to hit out at the Yankees, against my orders. Only when I threatened to have him court-martialled did he obey. The upshot of it all was that the Yankee group rode past our hiding place, in a small grove, without even suspecting that we were there, but it was obvious that they had been in some kind of a fight and we rode north once they had gone.

'It wasn't long before we discovered what had happened. One of our wagon trains, carrying about twenty thousand dollars of gold and bills had been attacked and almost all of the escort had been wiped out. I gave orders that the wagon, with the money still intact, was to be escorted back to our lines. That was when Carron showed himself in his true colours. That night, he talked the majority of the men into taking over the wagon for themselves, arguing that the war was nearly over and there wasn't a hope in hell that the South could win.'

'I think I'm beginning to get the picture,' nodded Dan. 'Go on.'

`I woke to find them preparing to move out. They'd hitched up the wagon and all of the horses, clubbed two of my men to death when they had refused to go with them. I tried to stop them but somebody knocked me over the head with a rifle butt and when I came round, I was lying there alone with handfuls of dollar bills stuffed into the pockets of my uniform. Seems they were only interested in the gold that wagon carried. That was easily convertible, even after the war, whereas Confederate money, as they'd foreseen, was useless.'

'Why didn't you report what had happened to your unit?' asked Dan.

'I don't know. Trafford.' The other ran the back of his hand over his forehead. 'I know I ought to have done that right away, but so many things happened that it wasn't possible.'

'What sort of things?'

'That marauding Union force came back that day and I was forced to hide up for three days in the wood while they camped in the valley just below. I was half dead from hunger and thirst by the time they finally rode off to the north. Then I tried to make it back to my lines, but I must have passed out somewhere along the way because when I next came to my senses, I was lying in a bed in a small ranch-house. There was an old couple there who nursed me back to health, but they'd found that money stuffed into my pockets and they'd heard about the Confederate force that had stolen their own gold and reckoned I was the leader of that bunch. They'd discovered my name from some papers I carried and when they thought I was asleep, I heard them talking with one of their hands, telling him to ride hell for leather to the Confederate lines and tell Colonel Bickford that the man they were looking for was Major Stacey and that he was at the ranch.'

'So you lit out of there as soon as you could. Was that it?'

The other nodded his head slowly. 'There was no other way open to me. If I'd stayed there and tried to defend myself, there would be too much damning evidence against me. I'd have been court-martialled and shot. Mebbe I was foolish and acted on the spur of the moment. The only defence I can put up is that I was still sick and didn't know just what I was doing. I couldn't see any way out for me and the one thought uppermost in my mind was that, perhaps, it might be possible for me to lie low until the war was over and by that time, everyone would have forgotten about me.'

'I see.' Dan rubbed his chin thoughtfully. Everything began to fit in. 'And of course, when you finally came here and built up this ranch, that fine herd of yours and this big ranch-house, you met up with the Carrons again. Only this time, they were a bunch of outlaws, preying on the Wells Fargo stages. They threatened to tell the army authorities about what had happened, knowing that with the wealth you had acquired here, it would be easy for them to claim that it came from the gold you had taken from that wagon and you wouldn't be able to prove otherwise.'

'Exactly. Now you see why I've given those orders to my men to shoot anyone who tries to trespass on my spread. I sent Mary east so that she would be out of the territory if the showdown came. I'd tried several times, unsuccessfully, to fight these men, but it was no use. Then, I must have given some indication of my worry in my letters to Mary, although I wasn't aware of it. I tried to make them sound the same as always, but she guessed. Probably womanly intuition, and came right back as soon as she could. Now she's in the middle of it all and I don't know which way to turn. I'd give anything to get free of this web I've woven for myself.'

'All you need do is give me the help I need. I'll see to it that the full and true story comes out.'

For a moment, there was a look of hope in the other's eyes and his back straightened imperceptibly in the chair. Then he shrugged. 'What can you do, Trafford? Those two men are still at large and very soon, they'll have every roughneck in the country behind them. Luke Carron will be hell bent on building up the biggest force of killers in the territory and when he does, he'll march on Carson or Shannon City.'

'Then we'll have to hit him before he gets that chance,' said Dan confidently.

'Have you any idea where he is?'

'Not at the moment. He tried to kill me this morning, but when Bateson arrived on the scene, he headed out north. I reckon he'll make it back to his hide-out in the desert. It's the only place in the territory where he feels reasonably secure.'

'I've heard of that place. The old silver mine workings. A bad place to try to attack. They could hold you off for days.'

Dan nodded slowly. 'I know. We hit them there a few nights ago, killed off most of the gang as you've probably heard. They aren't so invulnerable.'

'No, but the next time they'll be ready and waiting for you.'

'I've thought of that angle too. I reckon it would be easier if we were to wait for them to come to us.'

'What makes you so sure they'll do that. It would be like pushing their heads into a ready-made noose.'

Dan grinned widely, 'Don't get me wrong, Stacey. I'm not suggesting that they'll ride openly into Shannon City and shoot it out with me and the sheriff. I'm figuring that they'll arrive here very soon and when they do, I want to be here waiting for them.'

The other regarded him in silence for a long moment, his hands clasped in front of him on the desk. 'You may be right,' he said after a long pause. 'If they figure that things will get too hot for them at their hide-out they'll make for here and force me to put them up.'

'Can you trust all of your hands?'

'Yes, every one of them. Why?'

'Because we'll need every man we can get. I know the sheriff will want to be in on this too. I can get word through to him and we'll be here shortly after dark if you're willing to help us. Between us, I think we can stamp out this menace for good.'

The look of relief on the other's bluff features was plain to see. He got to his feet and several years seemed to have dropped from him during the past few minutes. 'I'm in with you, Trafford,' he said warmly, holding out his hand. 'It makes a man feel good to know that he's put the past behind him and is doing something decent for a change.'

'I'll get back to Shannon City right away,' promised Dan. 'Get your men together and tell them what to do. Right now, there's no telling how many men Carron might have. It's possible that I was trailed out here. If so, he'll know what's happened and he may come shooting. I'll do my best to get as many men out here as possible soon after dark.'

The other gave a quick nod. Going over to the door he opened it and said quickly: 'Bring Mister Trafford's horse round to the front of the ranch, Jake. He is going into Shannon City right now. When you've done that, I want to see you and all of the hands. There may be trouble tonight but this time, I know how to deal with it.'

'Right, boss.' There was a new expression on the other's face as he slipped Dan's gunbelt back to him. Five minutes later, Dan was riding hell for leather away from the ranch-house, towards the trail on the edge of the spread. There was no sign of Mary as he rode away but he guessed that her father would tell her the news the minute she returned.

He hit the trail fifteen minutes later and spurred the horse towards the town. The sun was lowering itself to the western horizon at his back as he rode, and lengthening shadows lay over the trail. He rode over the bridge and into the main street just as the sun went down and went straight up to the sheriff's office. Bateson came running out the moment he dismounted.

'What's wrong, Dan? Something happened at Stacey's ranch?'

'Not yet, but I've a feeling it's going to break any minute. Can you get some men together and ride back with me? I want to be there in case Carron and his men turn up tonight.'

'Sure, Dan. I'll have them ready in five minutes. In the meantime, pour yourself a cup of coffee, it's on the stove. I'll arrange for a fresh horse for you, that one looks plain tuckered out.'

Dan drank the scalding hot coffee gratefully. It made it possible for him to relax a little but the urgency was still there as he waited impatiently for Bateson to show up with the men. Finally, they rode into the street and he went out and swung himself swiftly into the saddle, showing no sign of the fatigue which was in his body. When they rode out, it was almost completely dark and the streets of Shannon City were almost deserted. They made fast time towards the Stacey ranch, cutting through the opening in the fence along the side of the trail, over the low pine-topped rise where Dan had been taken a few hours earlier and then down towards the ranch-house nestling at the bottom in the middle of the broad valley. There were several lights gleaming in the windows and a lot of bustling activity in the yard outside with men saddling horses and preparing to saddle up.

Dan noticed this with a feeling of surprise, rapidly turning to one of alarm. Something must have happened while he had been away. Stacey would never have made ready to let these men ride out if he intended to defend the ranch against attack. He dismounted on the run and went straight into the house. He found the rancher in the front room, pacing the floor. The other looked up swiftly as Dan came in.

'Thank God you've got back, Trafford,' he said hoarsely. 'I've been half out of my mind these past two hours.'

'What happened? Why are those men saddling up out there?'

'It's Mary,' the other blurted out swiftly. 'Carron has her. She rode out just before you came this afternoon. I'd no idea there might have been any danger otherwise I wouldn't have allowed her to go. But she's a headstrong girl, takes after her late mother, I suppose. When she hadn't returned by nightfall, I ordered two of my men to get saddled up to go to look for her. Once or twice in the past, her horse has thrown a shoe or lamed itself and she's had to walk back. But before the men left, I had a visit from Barton.'

'Barton! Didn't you hold him? He's in with the Carrons.'

'I know. He brought a message from Luke Carron. It said that they had Mary in their hands and that she would-n't be harmed in any way if I did exactly as Luke said. I was to take you by force when you came back and three of my men were to take you to the northern corner of the spread where Carron and his brother would be waiting. Then they would let Mary go.'

'I see.' The news had struck Dan with the force of a physical blow. It was the last thing he had expected, but inwardly he cursed himself for not having realized the possibility, especially when he felt so certain earlier that he had been trailed to the ranch and was depending on this to trap the Carrons there that night. Now it seemed that, once again, he had been a little too clever and the other had beaten him at his own game. He slid the gun in and out of its holster as he tried to think.

The mere fact that Stacey had told him this and had not taken him prisoner at gunpoint as Carron had ordered, meant that he could still trust the other to help him.

'When did they say your men were to take me there?' he demanded harshly.

'You're not thinking of giving yourself up, are you?' asked the other. 'I know I should ask it of you for the sake of my daughter. This fight has nothing to do with her. But this afternoon, you made me realize just how evil these men are and that everything possible has to be done to exterminate them. You'd never stand a chance if you went in alone.'

'I know,' Dan smiled grimly. 'But no matter what happens, they'll never let Mary go free. They want to hurt you for what you've done to them and this is their way of doing it.'

'What do you propose to do?' The other sounded dubious. 'I'll give you all the help I can. But if they don't intend to keep their part of the bargain they could have Mary locked away anywhere. You'd never find her in time.' He paused, licked his lips. Dan could guess at the turmoil that was raging inside the other's mind, could sense the desperate urgency about him. Inwardly, he himself knew that he was mainly to blame. Had he never come here, all this would never have happened. He was deliberately putting people into jeopardy just so that he might bring law and order to this territory.

With an effort, he pulled himself upright. 'I doubt whether they'll have taken her as far as their hideout in the desert. That would have meant cutting along the main trail and they would have run the risk of being spotted. I think they'll have holed up somewhere quite close at hand. Is there any place you can think of, at the moment, where they might consider themselves to be reasonably safe, particularly if they have a hostage?'

'There's the old Townsend ranch on the northern boundary of my spread,' said the other hesitantly. 'I know they were in the habit of hiding out there at times when the going got a little tough for them.'

Dan nodded. 'It's as good a place to start as any,' he agreed. 'I'll head in that direction. In the meantime, send a bunch of your boys out to the agreed meeting place. If there's anyone there, which I doubt very much, get them to say that I suspected something might happen like this and I never showed up. That ought to allay their suspicions for a little while without putting Mary into any more danger.'

'Very well, Trafford, I'll do as you say. But I only hope you know what you're doing. Her life is in your hands now.'

'I know,' he said soberly. He moved quickly to the door, climbed into the saddle and rode away into the darkness, aware of Bateson's curious gaze on him, knowing that a question had been forming on the sheriff's lips as he had ridden by. But time was precious if he was to have any chance at all of saving Mary's life. He rode quickly but cautiously, occasionally pausing to examine the ground, but even to his practised eye, there was no sign of a trail. There was a small stream running through the range and he followed it for a little while, knowing that this was the one which led from what had once been part of the old Townsend place to Stacey's spread. According to the records he had seen in Bateson's office that day, this had once been the boundary between the two spreads before old Townsend had died in a gun fight and his place had been taken over by Bob Stacey. Nobody lived in the old ranch-house now, according to Bateson, and it was gradually falling into ruin. But it would make an excellent hideout for the outlaws, particularly as the sheriff had been stressing the point it overlooked the stream and in daylight commanded an excellent view of the entire valley.

But he was approaching in darkness and although the moon would rise soon, it was still dark and the thick pasture muffled the sound of the horse's hooves so that it would be difficult for anyone to pick it out.

After a few minutes of riding along the bank of the stream, he struck off to the right, through rougher country where several large rocks dotted the ground and there were patches of coarse grass replacing the pleasant ground down in the valley. His keen gaze probing ahead, he spotted the cabin, perched on top of a wide outcrop of rock when he was still almost a quarter of a mile away. It looked to be deserted, but if they were there, he hadn't expected them to advertise their presence and he dismounted carefully, tethering the horse to a young sapling in the middle of a clump of bushes. Gently easing the gun from its holster, he crept forward, keeping his head low, scarcely daring to breathe. If the Carron brothers were there, they would be on the look out. On the other hand, one of them might have gone off to the appointed meeting place with Stacey's men, expecting him to turn up as their prisoner, knowing that whatever happened, Stacey would not dare take him prisoner for fear of losing his daughter. It was an excellent set-up, mused Dan as he slithered forward through the knee-high grass and weeds which had overgrown the place, but for one thing. They probably hadn't foreseen that he might come like this, alone and unheralded.

Crouching down less than twenty yards from the ranch, he paused and sized it up. There was an air about it that he didn't like. Then, very slowly, he manoeuvred himself into position until he lay crouched against the log wall just beneath the window. Now that he was so close, he was able to make out the faint light which flickered inside the place and he knew, with a sudden bounding of his spirits, that he was on the right trail after all.

He heard voices talking softly inside, but could not make out the words, although he felt certain that one of the voices belonged to a woman. Softly, he snaked his way around the cabin, every sense and nerve stretched to the utmost. Finally, he was satisfied. They had not posted a guard, unless that was him, in there, talking to Mary Stacey. Reaching the rear door, he pushed it gently, holding his breath as it creaked slightly on rusted hinges. Then he was inside, crouched low down, the gun out in his fist as he paused, listening. But there was no movement in the other part of the house and after a moment he released his breath in a soft sigh and slithered forward towards the door on the far side of the room. As he reached it, the sound of the voices came more strongly to his ears and he recognised Mary Stacey's voice. She spoke defiantly:

'You don't think my father will give in to your demands just to save my life, do you? You're finished here. Once the sheriff of Shannon City and Dan Trafford get on your trail, there isn't any place far enough for you to hide where you'll be safe.'

'Somehow I don't think so,' Barton's voice, harsh and angry. 'If Trafford isn't handed over to us tonight, they'll find your body in the morning like we promised. And pretty soon, there'll be more men joining us, men who can use a gun and aren't afraid of lawmen. Then we'll see who'll really run this territory. Shannon City and Carson are going to grow. There's plenty of silver and gold in those mines yet and that means prospectors, it means saloons and gambling joints and I mean to be in on the deal with Luke Carron and his brother.'

The girl said something more, but Dan had heard enough to convince him that there was only Barton in the other room with the girl and that the Carron brothers were out, hoping to pick him up from Stacey's men. With a tight grin on his face, he kicked open the door and stepped into the room, the gun fanning out to cover the startled sheriff who swung round at the sudden interruption. His right hand streaked for his gun the moment he saw who it was, but Dan's sharp and authoritative voice stopped the downward swing of his arm.

'Get your hand away from that gun, Barton, or I'll kill you right there,' he grated. 'I've waited a long time for this.'

'You won't get away with killing me, Trafford,' snarled the other, but even in the dim, flickering light of the oil lamp on the table, Dan could see the sweat which beaded the other's forehead and the look of stark fear in his close-set eyes.

'You're scared yeller, Barton,' he said softly, ominously. 'Drop that gunbelt and get over against the wall. Pronto!'

The other hurried to obey. His fingers fumbled with the

131

belt for several seconds before he managed to undo it and let it drop with a clatter to the floor. Then he stood over against the far wall with his hands raised over his head and his back to Dan. Swiftly, Dan went over and cut the ropes which bound Mary to the chair by the table. He held her for a moment as she swayed and would have fallen but for his arm.

'Think you can stand, Mary?' he asked softly.

She nodded. 'Oh Dan,' she said quietly, 'I thought you'd never find me. But those other two men. They've ridden off to my father. We've got to stop them.'

'No need to worry about them at the moment,' he reassured her. 'They think that your father has taken me prisoner and he'll be handing me over to them in return for you. We knew, of course, that they never intended to hand you back in exchange for me. They want to hurt your father for turning against them and this was the best way they knew of doing it.'

She shivered a little, clung to him for a moment, then pulled herself upright. 'I'm all right now, Dan,' she said softly, rubbing her wrists where the ropes had bitten cruelly into her flesh. 'What are you going to do with Barton?'

'That's something I haven't decided yet. It's a certainty that we can't leave him here to talk to Luke Carron when he gets back. I reckon we'll have to take him with us. I've no doubt that the citizens of Carson will be only too pleased to arrange a trial for him on a charge of murder. There's a rope waiting for him back there and he knows it, don't you, Barton?'

'You're bluffing, Trafford – and you know it,' said the other thickly. He turned his head a little, then squealed in mortal fear as Dan's gun jabbed hard into the small of his back.

'I think there's something you ought to know, Barton,' said Dan softly. 'It might explain a few things which have clearly been puzzling you. I'm not just a plain, ordinary cowpoke riding through Shannon City, with just a burning desire to put things right. I happen to be a Ranger, sent here specially to bring the Carrons to justice. And that goes for you too '

The other was silent at that. Dan could imagine what kind of thoughts were running through his head. He would clearly do everything possible to play for time hoping that the Carrons would arrive back in time to save him. Grimly, Dan stepped back and said sharply. 'Get moving, Barton. Out through the door and then turn right. I'm afraid there's only one horse so you'll have to walk, but the exercise ought to do you good.'

He turned as the girl swayed briefly against him and in that moment, Barton acted. He did a foolish thing, but with the knowledge that he had to do something if he was to have any chance at all of saving his life, he acted instinctively and without conscious thought. Side-stepping swiftly, he swept the lamp off the table and tried to run for the door. Without pausing to think, Dan snapped a shot at him, saw the other stumble and stagger back into the room, clutching at the wall by the door for support. In the same moment, the lamp smashed against the floor and there was an immediate gush of flame as the burning oil ran in blazing rivulets across the floor. The wood of which the building had been constructed was as dry as tinder after the long spell of hot, dry weather. It caught fire immediately, the flames leaping up the walls, catching at the bottoms of the musty, torn curtains still hanging over the windows, forming an impenetrable barrier between them and the door.

Swiftly, Dan thrust the girl behind him as he backed away. He could no longer see Barton because of the fire and smoke but there was no sound of movement above the crackling roar of the flames. If the other was unconscious, there was no hope for him. But somehow, he had to get the girl and himself out of what would soon become a raging inferno. The fire had gained a firm hold now and it was only a matter of minutes before the whole house went up in smoke. Not only that, but the blaze would be soon attracting unwelcome attention. Soon, the two Carrons would be on their way back here, empty-handed, and angry. Once they spotted the blaze they would come hotfooting it there with guns ready.

'The window,' said Dan tightly. 'It's our only hope.' He pointed, saw the girl hesitate, then she nodded. There was a smouldering patch of floor between them and the window, but it was their only avenue of escape and once she had made up her mind, she did not hesitate any more. Holding her handkerchief in front of her face, she ran quickly over the burning floor and a second later, Dan was beside her, coughing as the smoke bit cruelly at the back of his throat. Using the barrel of his gun, he smashed the pane of glass in the window, then helped the girl through. As she dropped to safety on the grass outside, he wriggled through himself, sucking the cool, refreshing night air down into his aching, smoke-filled lungs.

'We've got to get out of here fast,' he said, taking the girl's arm and hurrying her forward to where the horse stood waiting, 'Luke Carron and his boys will see that blaze miles away and they'll know what it means.'

'You think he has more men with him?' asked Mary as he helped her into the saddle. 'I thought you'd killed the rest of his gang?'

'We did, but there are plenty of roughnecks in the territory willing to throw in their hand with him. I doubt if he'd make a play like this if he wasn't sure he could count on plenty of guns.'

He swung himself up behind her, put the horse into a quick gallop. Gone was the need for silence now. The only thing that mattered was to get Mary back to the safety of her father's ranch. Once that was done, he could devote all of his energy to capturing or killing the outlaw brothers. Behind them, the conflagration was enough to be clearly seen, great gushing flames visible on top of the rocks, making a beacon of the old ranch which would stand out across the whole territory.

Deliberately, he skirted the pasture, reached the small

134

stream near its source and put the sorrel through it. They made slower time than he had when he had ridden out to the old Townsend place, but now the horse had two people to carry and besides, he was listening intently all the time for the druming of hooves in the distance which would tell him that the Carrons were returning, as fast as their mounts could carry them.

Not until five minutes later, did he hear what he had been listening for. By now, the moon had risen, round and full, still low on the eastern horizon, but giving enough light for him to pick out the riders who came over the ridge in the distance about a mile to the south-west. It was difficult for him to estimate how many there were, but his eyes narrowed as he watched them stream down the nearer slope. Too many of them for him to deal with, especially with the girl to take care of: and a glance was enough to tell him that if they remained where they were, they would be spotted as the others drew closer.

Still on the move, he turned his head quickly, spotted the clump of junipers that grew tall and bushy fifty yards to their right, a little way off the trail. Pulling around the horse's head he urged it towards them, ducking his head low as they rode beneath the overhanging branches. There he pulled up to tie up the sorrel. Here, away from the moonlight, it was almost dark which meant that he would be able to see those riders far more easily than they would be able to pick him out in the shadows.

Pulling the rifle from its scabbard, he stalked forward, cat-like to the edge of the trees, warning the girl to keep back near the horse in case of trouble. He did not think that the others had spotted him but at the moment he did not feel like taking chances. Keenly, he surveyed the rolling terrain which stretched away in front of him, gripping the rifle tightly in his hands. At first, he could see nothing of the men who had been headed in that direction and his first thought was that they had turned off the trail and cut across country, possibly hoping to come upon the burning ranch-house from the rear, intending to take

135

anyone who might be holed up there by surprise.

Then he saw them again as they rode up out of a narrow defile. Seven or eight men in single file and in the lead, spurring his mount forward cruelly, he recognized Luke Carron. Jeb was there too, hunched over the saddle. The other men riding with them he did not recognize, but he knew their type. Gunslingers who roamed the territory looking for an easy kill, content to work for anybody who asked no questions and paid them well. Luke Carron must have promised them plenty to join him, for they must surely have known by now that the whole territory was armed and ranged against them.

Very cautiously, he lifted himself up to his full height, depending upon the dark background of the trees to keep him hidden. That move brought the whole scene in front of him into stark focus. The men were still approaching, thundering along the trail. He flashed a glance elsewhere, but could see no more and guessed that this was the whole of the newly-formed Carron gang. It gave him an odd feeling of tension to realise just how quickly Luke Carron had seized the initiative again. A day or so earlier, he had been alone except for his brother and that crooked sheriff who now lay dead in the blazing inferno of the ranch-house. Now he had five or six men at the back of him, each a professional killer. As they rode closer, he saw that they were not on the watch for danger. They had not seen him or the girl and were clearly intent only on getting to that ranch as quickly as possible, realizing the worst. Probably Luke was already cursing the fact that he had been so supremely confident he had left only Barton behind to watch over the girl.

Dan tensed. Gently, he lowered the rifle to the ground and pulled the two guns from their holsters. The men would soon come within killing range of them and if even one of them spotted him, all of them would have to die. He felt sure of that, more certain of destiny than at any other time in his life. He didn't dare think of what they would do to the girl if he failed to shoot them all. Now they were fifty feet away and he could hear Jeb's harsh voice yelling savagely at the men immediately behind him.

But the men looked neither to right nor left as they thundered past on the trail. Dan stood within the protecting shadow of the trees and watched them narrowly until they were out of sight. On the hill in the distance, like a funeral pyre, the ranch-house suddenly erupted a gush of sky-soaring flame and sparks as the roof fell in. He shrugged, holstered the guns and bent to pick up the rifle. At least, he felt certain, that was the end of Sheriff Barton, a man who had disgraced the badge he wore, who had acted against the profession he had sworn to uphold. It was a fitting end to such a coyote, he thought savagely and felt only sorry that the two Carron brothers had not been trapped in that blaze with him. But they were still alive, and very dangerous. Once they discovered what had happened, he could guess at what they would do. Luke would be coldly furious, his scheming brain thinking ahead, working out some other diabolical plan, but knowing that this time, without the girl in his hands, he would be operating at a distinct disadvantage. Jeb, thinking only of anger and revenge, would advocate going out right away with all of the men and attacking the Stacey spread. Probably they would rustle off most of the cattle first, to draw off some of the defenders and then swoop on the ranch-house itself.

He tightened the girth of the saddle, then climbed up, pushing the rifle back into the scabbard.

'They've gone,' he said quietly. 'But once they discover what's happened, they will come back, thirsting for vengeance.'

'You think they'll attack my father's ranch, is that it, Dan?' Her voice was firm but troubled.

'I think so. Mebbe not tonight, but very soon.'

'If they do, we'll fight them,' she said with a defiant tilt to her chin. 'We'll show them that the Stacey's don't give in to outlaws. Besides, there are plenty of men there to help us.'

Dan nodded. He did not want to tell her that he doubted whether Bateson would be able to keep that posse there for long, before heading back to town.

CHAPTER SEVEN

GUNSMOKE VENGEANCE

HALF an hour later, they rode into the courtyard of the Stacey ranch, close on the heels of a bunch of men who rode in from the opposite direction. As Dan helped Mary from the sorrel, her father came out of the house. A moment later, Mary was in his arms. After a while, he looked across at Dan. There was a huskiness in his voice as he said: 'I don't know how I'll ever be able to repay you for what you've done tonight, Dan.'

Dan grinned at him. He threw Mary a quick glance and saw the faint blush on her face. 'Mebbe some day you'll be able to repay me, Mister Stacey,' he said meaningly, caught the look on the older man's face, saw the quick nod, and knew that the other had understood.

Then Dan was all business. 'We've got plenty to do yet though,' he said grimly. 'They'll have reached the old ranch-house by now and they'll know what happened there. If Jeb has his way they'll come riding here hell for leather. We passed them on the trail heading back. At least six of them, possibly seven. Seems he's hooked some gunslingers.'

'Think they'll ride with him against all of these men?' asked Stacey in mild surprise. 'If they do, they're fools.'

139

Dan looked at Bateson as the other spoke up, softly and seriously. 'That's something I reckon I ought to have mentioned before, Mister Stacey. With that band of outlaws roaming the territory, there's no telling where they'll strike. Sure, if Jeb has his way, they'll head straight for here. But somehow, I don't think he will get things as he wants them. And if I know Luke, he's a man who can bide his time.'

'Just what does that mean, Sheriff?' asked Stacey, looking hard at the other.

Bateson shrugged helplessly. 'It means that he'll probably figure he can attack the town with me and the rest of the boys out here waiting for him. I've got to protect the people there. That's the first part of my job. I'll have to get the posse back into Shannon City by dawn.'

'I see.' The rancher tightened his lips. 'Of course, you have your duty to do, Sheriff. I quite see that. I reckon that with the men I have here, we can hold the outlaws off if they do decide to attack.'

'I'll stay behind, Sheriff,' said Dan suddenly. 'You won't be needing me back in town.'

Bateson grinned. 'Somehow, I figured you'd say that, Dan,' he acknowledged. He turned to Stacey. 'Just how many men you got here?'

'Eight at the ranch. There are seven more out on the spread with the main herd but it would take a day to get word to them and another day for them to get here. I reckon we'll have to count them out of our reckoning.'

'I'm real sorry about this, Mister Stacey. I'll keep the men here until dawn. If they are going to attack, I doubt whether they'll do it in broad daylight.'

The balance of the night was a terrible building up of tension, a constant watch for an attack that never came. Dan spent most of it on the small rise near the ranch-house with two of the men, watching the trail which lay towards the north, but there was no sign of the outlaws. The fire in the distance, just visible from there, had long since died away and already the first grey streaks of dawn were beginning to show in the sky over the hills. He shivered in the cold night air and pulled his collar higher around his neck, The two men beside him stirred uneasily.

'Don't look as though they mean to come,' grunted one of them. 'Trail's empty as far as I can see. Mebbe they've decided to hit outa the territory fast.'

'Reckon they won't do that until they've finished what they started,' said Dan sharply, The other's words were just wishful thinking and could be dangerous. Thinking along those lines meant that soon, they would become certain that there would be no attack and then they would become over-confident, careless. Perhaps that was what Luke Carron was hoping for. If he could get the hands to think that there was no danger, especially if he could get Stacey to think that way, sooner or later, life at the ranch would return to normal, and it would be then that the Carrons would strike.

He stretched himself, threw another swift glance in the direction of the hills in the distance. Nothing moved out there in the half-light. The trail was just visible, stretching away through the lush pastures. Somewhere out there were the Carrons, knowing that he had beaten them once again at their own game, trying desperately to figure out how to retrieve their losses and destroy him.

They must know by now, he figured, that Stacey had told him the truth of what had happened all those years ago, and that they no longer had any hold over him. They could no longer look to him for unwilling help. A few minutes later, as they prepared to ride down to the ranch-house, they saw the posse come out and begin to saddle up. Dan tightened his lips just a shade. He eyed the ranch now through different, calculating eyes. There were too many trees close at hand, trees which would provide the outlaws with excellent cover when they came. From among them, they would be able to pour lead into the ranch-house from three sides with little danger of having to expose themselves to the return fire.

'Looks like the posse are riding out,' said the second man, swinging himself up into the saddle. He turned to Dan. 'You reckon there's any real danger of the Carron gang hitting Shannon City, Trafford?'

Dan pursed his lips. 'If Luke Carron has his way, perhaps. He's a crafty one. He knows he can afford to bide his time and he'll take every advantage of the situation. He doesn't allow his emotions to rule his head like Jeb. If we were dealing with Jeb, we'd know exactly what he intended to do and we could be ready for him. He'll strike out at the thing nearest to him, viciously and without thinking. He's like a rattler, determined to kill anything that hurts or angers him. Luke uses his brain and that makes him the more dangerous of the two.'

The other nodded. 'Could be that you're right,' he grunted. 'I say, we should get all of the boys together and ride out, attack the Carrons on their own ground without giving them the chance to ride against us.'

'And where would you go to find them?' asked Dan quietly. 'No sense in riding out to the old Townsend place. That was burnt down last night and you can bet your bottom dollar they aren't there any longer.'

'Then where do you fgure they are?'

Dan shrugged. 'The range is a pretty big place. They could be holed up anywhere. Reckon we could search all day and see neither hide nor hair of them.'

They reached the ranch just as Bateson was preparing to pull out. The sheriff gave him a quick, searching glance. 'We're leaving now, Dan,' he said quietly. 'If anything does happen and you can get a man through to Shannon City, we'll hot-tail it out here with every man I can get.'

'Thanks, Sheriff. We'll do our best to hold them if they do show up. I'm a bit worried about those trees being so close. Seems to me they could creep up on us unawares and get into a pretty tight position before we knew they were there.'

He rubbed his chin thoughtfully, 'Can't be helped, I

suppose. We'll just have to make the best of it.'

A few minutes later, the sheriff and his posse rode out and headed for the hills to the south, where they over-looked the trail back into town. After they had gone, Dan went around the ranch with Stacey, detailing the men to their positions, making certain that every side of the house was covered by at least two men with rifles. He wanted to have as much warning of the approach of the outlaws as possible. Fortunately, there was plenty of ammunition.

They settled down to wait. Two men were posted on top of the hill to keep a sharp look out on the trail. But the day passed and still Luke Carron had not made his play.

Bob Stacey asked thoughtfully: 'How can we be sure that he hasn't fled across the border now he knows that we're ready for him, Dan?'

'We can't be,' said the other, 'but I know both of these men. I was with them out there in the desert when they had me figured for Clayton, a wanted outlaw from back east, and I reckon I know how their minds work. They're completely unlike in their ways of figuring out things. Jeb would have been here before dawn, ready to shoot every-body in sight, even though it might have meant him being killed in the process. But Luke isn't like that. He thinks things out carefully before he makes a move and even though Jeb might try to force his opinion on the rest of the men there, I doubt if they'll listen. Luke's too smart to be caught on the wrong foot a second time. Besides, he means to kill me. He's gone to great lengths in the past to do that and I see no reason why he should pull out with his tail between his legs like a whipped cur just because things are against him. No, Bob, he'll come – and soon. But first, he'll try to get us to think that he has pulled out. Then, when we're least prepared for it, he'll ride against us.'

'Tonight, you figure?'

'Could be. I'd like to think he'll attack before nightfall, but I'm afraid he won't. He'd be spotted on the trail long before he gets here.'

The other nodded heavily. 'Let's get something to eat,'

he said gruffly, 'if'n you figure there's no danger at the moment.'

They went through into the kitchen where Mary had prepared a meal. Dan seated himself at the table and helped himself to turkey, beans and potatoes. The rising sensation of tension was still there in his mind, something which he knew he would be unable to throw off until it was all over. The knowledge that he and the rest of these men, even Mary, might be killed in the showdown which was coming, was at the back of his mind, but he deliberately kept it there, not wanting to think about it at that moment. Thoughts like that tended to slow up a man's reflexes just at the time when he needed them most.

Pushing away the plate he made himself a smoke and leaned back in the chair, forcing his body to relax, although it was impossible for him to relax his mind. There were too many thoughts streaming through it for him to be able to do that. He was trying to put himself into the outlaw leader's place, to think as he would be thinking at that very moment. What would be the best way to attack the ranch and be sure of killing off everyone in it. By now, the outlaws would know that the posse had ridden off, would probably have been watching the trail leading into town just to make sure. But they would also know there were at least half a dozen men inside the ranch, armed men, ready to fight. They would be cautious when they did come, hoping to get inside those trees out there under cover of darkness without being seen. Once there, they would be able to fire into the house from three directions.

Finishing his smoke, he pushed back his chair and got lithely to his feet. The rancher looked up at him in mild surprise. 'Reckon I'll take a look around outside and make sure that everything's in order,' he said easily. 'It's nearly dark and if they intend coming tonight, they may try sneaking up on us. I figure it might be possible to set up some kind of warning system.'

He was aware of Stacey's curious gaze on his back as he strode towards the door and went outside into the cool air.

In the store, he found several lengths of rope and several empty bean cans. Gathering these up, he made his way into the trees. It was an old Indian trick, but one which had proved useful in the past for giving a warning during the night.

Swiftly, he strung the rope out among the trees, tying it about four inches from the ground, then placed the empty cans, with stones inside them at intervals along it. Anyone crawling through the trees and brushing agaist one of these ropes would make enough noise to waken the dead. And if they tried to come through on horseback, intending to ride down on the ranch, they would be in for trouble. The ropes were at just the right height to bring a horse crashing down, unseating its rider.

At last, he was satisfied and went along to where the two guards were still on top of the low rise. He found them alert, watchful. They spun quickly at his soft, cat-footed approach, then lowered their rifles and relaxed.

'Anything stirring out there?' he asked tightly. They shook their heads.

'Nothing so far, Mister Trafford. When do you reckon they'll make their play?'

'Any time after dark. They'll be somewhere out among the hills yonder, waiting until nightfall before riding in.' They waited there until it was too dark to see the trail in the distance, then moved down to the ranch-house. Stacey looked across at him, an unworded question in his eyes. Dan nodded. 'They'll be here pretty soon if they're going to come at all. But at least we ought to get a little warning once they hit those trip-ropes I've laid among the trees.'

'We'll be ready for them,' nodded the rancher. He seemed to have attained a new stature now, a man who had faced up to the nightmare which had been haunting him for years and who knew that he had the will and the courage to fight it out to the bitter end, no matter what that might be. Dan watched him for a moment with a feeling of satisfaction. The other would redeem himself this night, he felt sure. As for the rest of the men, they may not have been professional killers like those who rode with the Carron brothers, but they knew how to handle their guns and they would shoot to kill as soon as the outlaws made their attack.

Outside, it grew darker and he ordered the lights to be put out in the room. It enabled them to see more clearly in the darkness and also made it more difficult for the outlaws to hit them. For a long moment, he stood beside the window, staring moodily out into the night. The trees in the near distance were dark and ominous. He took out his six-guns, checked them carefully, then held them ready. In his mind's eye, he could visualize the outlaws dismounting in the distance so as to give no warning of their approach, coming in on foot towards the trees. If there were only the seven or eight of them, things would not be so bad, but if Carron had managed to persuade more to join him, it was possible they would find themselves to be hopelessly outnumbered. For one moment, he debated whether or not to send a man into town to warn the sheriff, then decided against it. If the outlaws were out there, close at hand, the man would be shot before he had ridden half a mile unless he were fantastically lucky; and it was just possible that Luke Carron had foreseen such a move and would let the man get through, waiting for the posse to show up, before hitting it back into town. He shuddered as he realized the pillage and slaughter that this gang of cut-throats would carry out in an unprotected town.

He heard Stacey at the other window in the room suddenly hiss a warning. His head jerked up instantly and he cursed himself for day-dreaming at a time like that.

'What is it?' he whispered sibilantly.

'I thought I heard horses. Not close, somewhere out there beyond the hills.'

Dan listened intently, but could hear nothing. The night seemed completely silent and in the dim shadows nothing moved.

'I don't hear anything. Are you sure, Bob?'

'Pretty sure, but I don't hear it now.'

146

Dan knew better than to question the other's judgment. It was more than likely that he had heard horses, but that the outlaws had halted them at what they considered to be just out of earshot from the ranch and were coming the rest of the way on foot, knowing that they had plenty of time in which to make their play.

'Everybody keep their eyes open from now on,' he advised. 'If you hear anything out there among the trees, shoot to kill. If they know that we're alert and waiting for them, they may pause to consider. And if we can keep them there until daylight we stand a good chance.' He glanced about him, then over at Stacey.

'Where's Mary, Bob?'

'Back in the kitchen, I reckon,' said the other. 'She's got a rifle and one of the boys with her. If'n you think she ought to be locked away safely, then I guess you'd better go through there and talk with her. I've tried my damnedest but she takes after her mother; headstrong and determined. She won't listen to me.'

Rising to his feet, Dan went swiftly into the kitchen. Mary was close by the darkened window, the rifle in her hands. She turned swiftly as he came in.

'Mary! Don't you know that these men are killers? This isn't going to be a game. They'll shoot you just as much as any one of us. Get into one of the bedrooms where you'll be safe and leave the shooting to the men.'

'Not on your life,' declared the girl hotly. 'I can handle this rifle as well as any man as my father will testify and I intend to stay here and get myself one of those outlaws. If my father had had a son instead of a daughter, he would have been here to fight. Well, I don't see why I should be any different.'

Dan tried pleading with her, but finally was forced to give up and go back into the front room. Before he went, he said to the man standing at the other window. 'Keep a watch on her, Jake.'

'Don't worry, Mister Trafford. I'll see to it that she's all right.'

147

Dan hoped that he would be able to keep his word, but it was with a heavy heart and a worried frown on his lean, handsome features that he went into the front room and joined Stacey. The rancher gave him a quick look, raising his brows a little. Dan shook his head. 'She wouldn't listen to me either,' he said quietly. 'Her mother must have been some woman if Mary takes after her.'

'She was,' agreed the other quietly. 'When she died, I thought that everything was finished here. I didn't see how I could have gone on, I think it was only because of Mary that I managed to pull through that bad time.' He opened his mouth to say something further, but it was never said for at that precise moment, there was a sudden racket from among the trees directly in front of them, the sharp rattle of cans and a sudden, muffled curse as a man tripped over the ropes laid in the undergrowth.

Swiftly, instinctively, Dan brought up both guns and thumbing back the triggers fired swift shots into the trees.

The din of gunfire suddenly erupted around the house and he realized that most of the outlaws had succeeded in getting close enough without blundering into the trip-ropes. Had it not been for that clumsy-footed man out there, they might have crept up on them, unseen and unheard.

He opened his mouth to shout a warning through to the men in the other rooms, but it was not needed. The roar of answering fire told him that the rest of the men were alert to the danger.

A moment later, there was a pause in the firing from the trees. Dan ceased firing and ordered the others to do like-wise. They waited. After a moment, he heard Luke Carron's voice calling from in front of him.

'Can you hear me, Stacey?'

'I can hear you, coyote,' shouted Bob Stacey loudly. 'What have you got to say? Whatever it is, get it over with and then make your play. We're ready for you and the rest of those rattlers with you.'

'I got no call to shoot it out with you, Stacey. Just turn

148

over that lawman you've got in there, the one who calls himself Trafford and we'll be on our way. I promise that we'll ride out and not bother you again. If you don't, then we'll come in there and kill every one of you, including your daughter. I've got ten men out here with me, all of them itching to move in. I can't promise to hold 'em back much longer.'

'I've had enough of your promises, Carron,' yelled Stacey tightly. 'You've bled me white these past few years and for something I didn't do. But I've explained all that to the law.'

'You're being a fool, Stacey.' There was a faint note of impatient exasperation in the outlaw's tone. 'This is the last chance I'm going to give you. Turn Trafford over to us and the rest of you will be unharmed. He's the only man I want. The rest of you mean nothing to me.'

The only answer he got was a shot from Stacey's gun. Dan saw the dark figure melt back into the trees and tensed himself for the fusillade of shots which he knew would follow. He was not disappointed. Bullets crashed into the wall close by the window and he could see the muzzle flashes of their guns, brief stabbing flames in the darkness. One man broke cover, a fleeting shadow racing forward in an attempt to throw himself down in the long grass a few yards from the front of the house. But he had only gone two paces before a couple of leaden slugs hit him in the chest and he went down on his face, unmoving.

'Once they pin us down they may try to rush us,' he said tightly, 'Better make every bullet count if they do.'

'I'm ready for them,' said the other grimly. He fired at a tall shape moving among the trees, missed, but the man slumped down swiftly, off balance as the bullet hummed close to his head.

The volume of gunfire increased sharply over the next few minutes as the outlaws poured everything they had into the ranch-house. Dan fired swiftly at running shapes which were visible for a few seconds as they fled from cover to cover, but hit none of them. There had to be some reason why they were wasting all of that lead, he reasoned, but at the moment, he failed to see what it was. Obviously there was a plan being built up against them, but he could not figure it out.

Then, suddenly, there was a yell from Stacey. The big man leapt back bringing up his rifle as the glass in the window shattered and a tall figure leapt through into the room. One blow felled the rancher and the outlaw was inside the room, his gun swinging on Dan. Instinctively, without pausing to take proper aim, Dan fired. Both guns crashed at the same time but the other had been too hurried, had been slightly off balance when he had hit the floor, going down into a half crouch to present a more difficult target. His bullet hummed past Dan's shoulder and thudded into the wall behind him. Dan's own slug caught the man high in the shoulder and he reeled back under the impact of lead. Flopping down on to his stomach, the outlaw brought up his gun again, thumbing back the trigger. Lowering his own gun, Dan pulled the trigger, heard the ominous click as the hammer hit an empty chamber. There was a wolfish grin on the other's features as he pushed himself awkwardly to his feet and advanced into the centre of the room. As he came forward, Dan recognised the leering face of Jeb Carron. The outlaw's lips were drawn back into a snarl of triumph as he realized that he had the lawman at his mercy with an empty gun in his hand.

'This is where you get it, Traffford,' he gritted harshly. 'I've been waiting a long time for this. Luke says to take you alive, but that ain't for me. I want to see you dead. Then I know that we'll be finished with you for good.' His finger tightened on the trigger and although he staggered a little, blood showing high on his shirt where Dan's last bullet had ploughed deep into his shoulder, he still came forward. Dan tensed himself, waiting for the leaden impact of the bullet, but when the shot came, thundering in the confined space of the room, he felt no hurt, merely heard a sudden coughing grunt. Opening his eyes, he saw to his surprise that Jeb Carron was sliding forward, his right hand clawing feebly at the top of the table as he tried to remain on his feet. His mouth was hanging slackly open and his eyes were wide and glazed. The gun slipped from his nerveless fingers and hit the floor a second before he did.

Lifting his eyes, Dan glanced instinctively towards the doorway. Mary Stacey stood in the open doorway a smoking rifle in her hands. Very slowly she looked up at him, her face a pale blur in the darkness.

'I heard the glass breaking and came back to see what had happened,' she said in a faintly strangled tone. 'Who is it? One of the outlaws?'

'Jeb Carron,' he said softly. 'I'm glad you were right when you said you could handle that rifle. You saved my life.'

'Jeb Carron.' For a moment, the girl came forward and stood looking down at the dead outlaw stretched at her feet. Then she noticed her father lying near the window and ran forward with a sharp cry.

'It's all right, Mary,' Dan said quickly. 'He's just out cold. Jeb hit him over the head with his gun as he came through the window. He wanted me, not your father, that's why he didn't pause to shoot him.'

Going down on one knee, he examined the rancher quickly, then turned to the girl. 'He'll be OK in a few moments, Mary. You'd better get back into the kitchen, while I keep watch here. They'll try to rush in very soon.'

Even as he spoke, several shots hummed through the splintered glass of the window and hit the wall on the opposite side of the room. Without another word, Mary got to her feet, keeping her head low, and slipped out through the door. Dan leapt back to the window, loading his guns as he went. Three men were running forward from the trees, almost at the edge of the courtyard. Evidently, they had taken the sudden cessation of fire from the window to mean that Jeb had succeeded in his attempt to kill them and that it would be safe for them to advance.

Throwing lead swiftly, he saw two of the men topple on to their faces just beyond the fence at the courtyard's edge. The third hit the dirt, tried to wriggle away when he found there was no cover there. Dan's third bullet hit him in the leg and he screamed shrilly before the next slug hammered into his chest.

A few minutes later, when Bob Stacey recovered consciousness and sat up, rubbing his head gingerly, the fire from the trees had died away to only an occasional shot.

'I reckon we've beaten them off,' said Dan tightly. 'I guess it's time we took the initiative. Can you get the boys together and we'll ride out and run them down before they manage to slip away.'

'Sure, Dan.' The other was still dazed, but the urgency in the lawman's voice got through the fog in his brain and he went into the other rooms. A few bullets cut through the air as they went out into the darkness and there was a sudden movement among the trees. At the edge of the courtyard they stumbled over the three men that Dan had killed and there were two more near the corral. One of the men reported that three had been killed and one wounded on the other side of the house. Including Jeb Carron, lying back there in the house with Mary's bullet in his back, that meant there could be only one man still alive. Even though they had examined every man carefully, there was no sign of Luke Carron. Dan tightened his lips and hitched his gunbelt higher about his waist. He had expected that the other had kept himself well in the background, out of danger, until he knew how the gunfight was progressing. Now that he knew it was finished, that his brother was either dead or badly wounded, the only thought in the outlaw's mind would be to get out of the territory as fast as a horse would carry him. Swiftly, Dan wheeled, ran to the corral and hitched up one of the horses. He was in the saddle and heading for the open gate when he heard the drumming of hooves fading into the distance. Luke had made it back to his horse and was pulling away fast into the distance. The other men around him were getting the horses rounded up ready for pursuit but he did not wait for them. He had the feeling that this was now something personal between him and Luke Carron. If anyone was to go after the outlaw it was to be him.

Setting the horse to a swift gallop, he headed for the hills, deliberately skirting the trees and cutting down into the valley beyond. In the flooding moonlight, he thought he could make out the figure of the outlaw in the distance, heading for the hills. Once he got into those rocks, he could lose himself for days and it would be the devil's own job trying to find him.

Swiftly, the horse leapt forward as he spurred it onward. He was not used to using a horse cruelly, but there was something driving him now which would not be stilled until either he or Luke Carron was dead.

Gradually, he began to overhaul the other, narrowing the distance between them. He was close enough now, to be certain of the identity of the man in front of him. Once Carron turned in the saddle and snapped a couple of shots behind him, but they went wild and Dan continued to edge forward. The other's lead had been too great however for Dan to catch up with him before he hit the rocks and by the time he came within shooting distance, Carron was already setting his horse at the narrow, rocky trail which led up into the hills. Here, there was plenty of cover and as Dan had expected, the other vanished among the boulders before he could get a snapshot at him.

He pulled up swiftly, eyes alert. Seconds later, a shot hammered into the dust just in front of the horse. It reared savagely, then calmed. Swiftly, he threw himself out of the saddle, wormed forward into the rocks. He knew now, with a sudden certainty that Carron was not going to try to make a break for it, that the other had realized he was trapped and the only thing to do now was to shoot it out with Dan while he held the slender advantage.

Dan looked about him swiftly, then glided towards a pile of boulders which stood out from the ground twenty feet above him. His feet scraped on the slippery rock and a couple of bullets ricocheted off them, causing him to duck swiftly. Dan tried to figure out exactly where the other was. Desperately, he crawled forward, guns out and ready, eyes piercing the shadows thrown by the moonlight. Carron could be crouched down in any one of them, waiting for him to show himself.

He raised his gaze higher, then stiffened slightly as he made out the shape of the outlaw's horse, standing on a narrow trail about thirty yards above him. Swiftly, he took deliberate aim, threw a couple of slugs in front of the animal and then another behind it. As he had hoped, the horse suddenly reared up, lunged forward at the bridle holding it to an outjutting branch and careered away along the trail.

'Better give yourself up, Carron,' he called loudly. 'You don't stand a chance of getting out of here alive unless you do. Not with your horse gone.'

'Damn you, Trafford. Come in and get me.' There was an ungovernable anger in the outlaw's tone now and another shot smashed into the rocks close to where Dan lay. He grinned tightly to himself. By yelling like that, the other had given away his position.

Very carefully, he eased himself forward over the rocks, keeping his head well down, his arms extended slightly in front of him. For a long moment there was silence over everything, a deep and clinging silence which seemed like a pressing shroud. Slowly, he moved himself around the place where the outlaw lay, until he had reached a point just above and to one side of him. He peered around the edge of a boulder, then picked up a small rock and hurled it with all his strength far over to the left of the hidden man.

It struck the rocks with a loud sound and went bouncing away down the slope. Instantly, Carron fired, sending shot after shot after the falling stone. A moment later, there was the harsh and unmistakable click of the hammer striking an empty chamber. The other was just thrusting shells into the gun when Dan came up on to the rock immediately behind him.

'Better not move, Carron, or I'll fill you full of lead,' he said softly. 'And don't try to turn round because I won't hesitate to shoot you in the back. A snake like you doesn't deserve to live.'

'Just as I thought,' sneered the other. 'The big Dan Trafford, lawman. Has to shoot a man in the back because he's afraid to face up to him.'

'Throw down that gun, Carron, and then get on to your feet,' Dan snapped. 'I'm taking you into Shannon City to face trial. I think you can guess what the outcome of that is going to be.'

For a moment, he thought the other intended to disregard his order. Then the six-gun rolled down the slope and Carron pushed himself upright, turning slowly. He looked straight at Dan with a wide sneer on his thin lips. 'I suppose you figure that you've won, Trafford,' he said harshly. He shook his head. 'This isn't the finish for me.'

'Don't fool yourself, Carron. This is the end of the line for you. The rest of your men have been killed back there. Jeb has been shot. There's only you left to face trial! Now get moving and don't try anything funny.'

He climbed down the rock and moved towards Carron and it was then that the outlaw made his move. Even though he had been prepared for it, Dan was taken slightly by surprise by the speed at which the man's hand jerked towards the inside of his frock coat, his hands closing over the small Derringer there. He had it halfway, out of his pocket when Dan pressed the trigger. For a moment, the other remained upright, one hand pawing the air in front of him blindly, the other dropping to his side. There was an expression of stark amazement on his features in the moonlight. Then he swayed forward and toppled on to his face at Dan's feet.

Feeling for the pulse, Dan was finally satisfied that the other was dead. Getting him over his shoulders, he carried him back to his horse and threw him across the saddle, tying the outlaw's body down with the lasso. Then he rode back towards the Stacey ranch.

'So you finally caught up with him, Dan,' said Bateson, the following morning. 'I rode in here with some of the boys just in case we were needed, but I can see that you managed fine by yourselves. At least it saves us the expense of a trial and they got no more than they deserved.' He turned to Stacey. 'I figure you can be thankful to Dan here, Bob. If it hadn't been for him, you might still have had those outlaws on your neck.'

'I reckon I know how much I owe to Dan,' said Stacey warmly. 'I figure that Mary has a say in that too, but I know she'll want to say that for herself,'

'What are you figuring on doing now, Dan?' asked Bateson, turning to the other. 'I know your work here has finished, but I guess the Rangers could let you go, especially as we need a sheriff over at Carson. I figure you'll just about fill that post.'

'Thanks, Sheriff. But I guess that isn't for me,' Dan saw the look of disappointment on Mary's face as she stood in the doorway, and grinned. 'But you're right about the Rangers being willing to release me. I'm sending off a message by telegraph as soon as I get into town.'

'Then what do you figure on doing, Dan?'

'Well, I've had a long talk with Bob here and it seems he's been looking for a partner around the place. I reckoned we might rebuild that old Townsend place out there and if I'm to marry Mary, it's time I started out getting some cattle for myself.'

'I reckon you'll have enough to start a fine herd,' said Stacey, nodding, as Mary came into the room and took Dan's arm. 'Mary here has been putting something by towards a herd of her own for some years. There ought to be close on a hundred head or so by now.'

There was a silly, smug grin on Bateson's face as he turned and went towards the door.

Shannon City Breakout

Gun-law ruled in Shannon City, a small frontier settlement near the Texas border, when Sheriff Bateson appealed to the Rangers for help. Daily stagecoaches were being held up, and their passengers robbed. The marauding gunhawks shot any who dared resist. Spearheaded by the powerful Carron gang, they were fast reducing the territory to ruin.

Fearful of the terrible vengeance of the Carron gang, the local townspeople were too scared to help Dan Trafford when he rode into Shannon City, for what could one man do, unaided, against seven fast and ruthless killers? But with characteristic courage and grim determination, Dan struck back at the gang, and finally succeeded in whittling down their number until only two remained: two savage men who swore vengeance upon him.

When the bloody showdown came, could Dan outdraw the killers?